MY
IMMACULATE
ASSASSIN

Also by David Huddle

Dream Sender, poems, 2015
The Faulkes Chronicle, novel, 2014
Black Snake at the Family Reunion, poems, 2012
Nothing Can Make Me Do This, novel, 2011
Glory River, poems, 2008
Grayscale, poems, 2004
La Tour Dreams of the Wolf Girl, novel, 2002
Not: A Trio: A Novella & Two Stories, 2000
The Story of a Million Years, novel, 1999
Summer Lake: New & Selected Poems, 1999
Tenorman, novella, 1995
A David Huddle Reader, stories, poems, and essays, 1994
Intimates, stories, 1993
The Nature of Yearning, poems, 1992
The Writing Habit, essays, 1992
The High Spirits: Stories of Men & Women, 1989
Stopping By Home, poems, 1988
Only the Little Bone, stories, 1986
Paper Boy, poems, 1979
A Dream With No Stump Roots In It, stories, 1975

MY IMMACULATE ASSASSIN

DAVID HUDDLE

TUPELO PRESS
North Adams, Massachusetts

Library of Congress Catalog-in-Publication data available upon request.
ISBN paperback: ISBN-13: 978-1-936797-77-6

Cover and text designed by Ann Aspell.

First edition: September 2016.

Epigraph: Excerpted from *Stranger Music* by Leonard Cohen.
Copyright © 1993 Leonard Cohen. Reprinted by permission of McClelland
& Stewart, a division of Penguin Random House Canada Limited.

Tupelo Press
P.O. Box 1767
243 Union Street, Eclipse Mill, Loft 305
North Adams, Massachusetts 01247
Telephone: (413) 664–9611 / Fax: (413) 664–9711
editor@tupelopress.org / www.tupelopress.org

Tupelo Press is an award-winning independent literary press that publishes
fine fiction, non-fiction, and poetry in books that are a joy to hold as well as
read. Tupelo Press is a registered 501(c)(3) non-profit organization, and we
rely on public support to carry out our mission of publishing extraordinary
work that may be outside the realm of the large commercial publishers.
Financial donations are welcome and are tax deductible.

"Give me Christ,
or give me Hiroshima."

—LEONARD COHEN

CONTENTS

MY
IMMACULATE
ASSASSIN

THE FUTURE

"Pick a person," she said, very quietly. "Any person."

I knew I was under the influence of how lovely she was, but what she was asking me to do sounded almost reasonable. We were splitting a tiramisu at the Trattoria, and this wasn't the conversation I thought we'd be having. I'd planned to ask her to have lunch with me in the East Building on Sunday and then to have a look at the Lichtenstein retrospective.

"And you will…?" Was I really going to put this into words?

"No," she said. Then she snorted. "It can't be condensed into subject-verb-object. 'It will happen.' That's how to say it. That's how to think about it, too." Her face was cheerful.

"All right," I said. "I misspoke, and I apologize. What I meant to say was, 'This person will….'?"

"Yes," she said. "That's closer to how it will be. And if we want to speak of *agency*, unfortunately the agent in question will be you. Because *you* will be—or will have been—the decider."

When we looked at each other then, I couldn't really say what our mood was. She had of course once been in the chain of command of the person who made "the decider" into a nationally laughable term. I of course now understand that with Maura's aid that man could have become a decider in a way that would have stopped the laughing.

I set down my fork even though I hadn't finished my half of the tiramisu. "I'm not a decider," I said. I sighed and blinked. "I just really don't want to do this."

"Of course you don't." Now her face had become stone neutral. "And of course you don't have to." She shrugged. It was a very appealing shrug. It said, *I know you're weak, and I forgive you.*

"But you think I will," I said.

Her tight smile made it clear that she felt sorry for me. But then I saw something else in her face. This really mattered to her. She put down her fork and shivered ever so slightly. She was willing herself not to look vulnerable. I reminded myself that she had taken an extraordinary risk in confiding in me.

The longer our stare-down continued the more it morphed into a gaze of mutual affection. When she finally broke it, I knew she did so for my sake. To be courteous. "There's no hurry," she said quietly. "No hurry whatsoever."

"I hope I won't be getting back to you," I said.

She shrugged again, but then she met my eyes, and this time her smile wasn't forced.

"Should we go?" I asked. She nodded, and when I had called for the check and signed the credit slip, we sat quietly for a moment. When we stood up, we were almost in unison. I'd have been hard put to say exactly what had transpired between us, but I was definitely feeling the weight of it.

Outside the restaurant, we held each other more tightly than we had before. I was the one who let go first.

⌘

"It wasn't something I was trying to find out, and the instant I knew it, I wanted to give it back," Maura had told me, shaking her head, miserable even in remembering the day, the hour, the minute. We were in her apartment. She went on to assert that it wasn't fair how the knowledge came to her, because in her opinion it was something so obvious it hardly even qualified as science. "There are three facts that anybody who got through college probably knows. One of them has to do with drones, another has to do with cell phones, and the third is basic physics. Well, you need a little chemistry, too, but not much. You imagine these pieces of common knowledge configured in a certain way, and you've got it."

"But isn't it that *certain way* that qualifies you to be the one?" I asked. "Your background, your ability to look at the world as no one else looks at it? If it's so obvious, then why are you the only person to see it? Find it, stumble on it, whatever you want to call what you found out." I was impatient with her that first time we talked about it. I could see that my impatience hurt her feelings.

She stood up and stepped over to the window, her back to me. "I don't know. I do know that it's out there. It's right in front of our eyes—everybody's eyes. And it can't be too long before it occurs to somebody else like it did me. Out of the blue. Flash of light." Her voice was sad. She turned to face me. "A cabbie in Brooklyn. A melon farmer in California. A homeless woman in Boston. Anybody can

6

just be walking along and suddenly know it. I'm here to tell you—you don't have to be looking for it."

⌘

I didn't entirely believe Maura—that it was available to anyone. She in fact had a doctorate in aerospace engineering from MIT. In addition to an undergraduate degree in theology from Cornell and a couple of years of med school at Johns Hopkins, with some other esoteric credentials. Which was why at age thirty-five, she worked in DC alongside very high-end and wonky people in the technical research division of what they call "the intelligence community." As an undergraduate at Cornell, she had earned the nickname "Stealth Woman" for maintaining such a low-profile presence that her professors and her classmates hardly noticed her, while people in her classes kept on hearing about this student who was doing extraordinary work. Nobody quite knew which among them was the genius. Maura told me she'd have never been found out, if a professor hadn't read to his class a paragraph she'd written in a paper about black holes and the information they might or might not contain.

If IQ were all there were to Maura, there'd have been nothing all that special about her. She would have been the first to say so. On our first date she told me that Earl Scruggs was every bit as smart as Albert Einstein. "'Foggy Mountain Breakdown' is as much of an achievement as E equals M-C squared. It's just that when Scruggs talked, he sounded like he had a wad of chewing tobacco in his jaw."

She admitted she was smart, she said just being smart was not remarkable. It took me a while to accept her modesty as genuine. Again and again she was surprised to find out that not everybody was as knowledgeable as she was. "You don't know that?" she would say, surprised and amused, when I asked her the name of a tree, a bird, a piece of classical music, a city in northern Japan. Every morning I spent a couple of hours with the *New York Times*, she spent ten minutes, and you can guess which one of us remembered it well enough to quote whole sentences from every section.

Maura even denied another quality of her mind that I think set her apart from everybody else. I was aware of it for months before I tried to name it. I made her laugh out loud when I told her I'd decided she was a spiritually resonant human being.

"I'm a passionate atheist," she said. "My faith is called science. You could say I'm a spiritual vacuum."

"Well, only someone who would completely deny it could possess that quality." I was kidding with her, but after I spoke—and after she gave me a long inquiring stare—I decided I might be right. A truly spiritually resonant person wouldn't be able to see it in herself.

But what I meant was that Maura had an intuitive regard for just about everything. Birds, animals, buildings, grass, manure, subways, advertisements, insects, even nutty politicians. It was not like she tried to be that way, it's just that she walked around a little bit in awe of everybody and everything she encountered. A freaked-out meth-head shouting insults to pedestrians on 42nd Street—Maura walked away from him saying, "Wow, that guy is really something! Did you hear what he called me?!" The way you'd talk about somebody you respected. She was the opposite of most of the smart people I've known—who have little regard for anybody who isn't brilliant.

But if one person on the planet had to come into possession of a way, without being physically present, to bring about the death of any human being so that it looked like the person had died of natural causes—if there had to be somebody to find out how to do that, over and above every other living person, I'd have preferred that it be Maura Nelson from Clarksville, Tennessee. The nerdy lady with a little twang in her voice.

⌘

"Easier than pie," she said when she confessed her secret to me. "By a long shot. Even if you use store-bought crust, pie's a tough assignment."

I shook my head. We were drinking prosecco—okay, we were tipsy and mildly happy—in my apartment. For the record, it was the only time I'd ever seen Maura close to drunk, and this was only because of what she called "converging forces." She and I had been seeing each other for weeks, but she had been so reticent and distracted that I was ready to give up on her. So I decided to try to get her tipsy around the same time she apparently decided she needed to do something to let me know she was indeed interested in me. Okay, so that was one of the forces. Another one was the prosecco, which Maura had never tasted and which she really liked. But the main factor was what she knew and what she'd done with it—the hurricane, the earthquake, the tornado that she'd been carrying around in her mind for about a month.

"No special equipment required," she said. "The only

easier method would be to have it happen just by closing your eyes and making a wish. You don't have to be anywhere near the individual. Not even on the same continent."

Twenty-eight days ago Bashar al-Assad had dropped dead while showering in the presidential residence in Damascus. His heart had stopped beating. Syria was in a state of extreme upheaval, but the whole world was pretty happy about not having to deal with that son of a bitch anymore. There wasn't even an attempt to blame the death on Israel or the U.S.

This night of our tipsiness Maura and I stayed up late, talking, drinking—kissing every now and then but cautious in that regard. We were both too full of what was transpiring in the world as well and we were only tentatively realizing that affection and desire had come down upon us. She insisted on phrasing it as "perhaps in love," because she claimed she'd had no previous experience with relationships. I believed her about this, because as a kisser she was a beginner. She said it would take her a while to determine (her word) if love was what we were in. The love issue and her clandestine contribution to the death of al-Assad were already too much for her to absorb that evening. She had no interest in taking on the issue of losing her virginity at age thirty-nine. I liked it that she'd never had sex—I knew she was telling the truth about that. There are worse ways for people to strike up a romance.

Maura went out of her way to look neutral. She used zero make-up and wore unremarkable clothing. That evening when I accused her of stifling her own beauty, she told me, "A standard human being, that's what I want to look like." I'm certain she believed her looks were average.

She was mostly right. It was just that if she was at ease or amused or excited, then her face became lively and suddenly you found her extremely appealing.

A little later that evening when I was about to drive her back to her place, I told her, "You could pass for beautiful."

She liked that enough to give me a very affectionate hug. "I often pass as a librarian," she said.

"Ha," I said. She and I had met in the Bethesda county library when I mistook her for someone who worked there and asked her which way to the periodicals room.

⌘

"I've done this just that one time. And the only reason I'm willing to do it again is because I want another person to be in on it with me. And sharing the anxiety that goes with it. I could be accused of committing a war crime," she told me with more than a little passion in her voice. Then she murmured, "I almost *want* to be brought up before an international court just to see how it would play out."

We were quiet then. I knew what was passing through her mind. The world wasn't ready for what she'd found out, and never would be. Humankind would extinguish itself.

"I'm not going to tell you the way it works. You shouldn't have to carry that burden. But I'm going to ask you to make the decision about someone else. A second test case. All you have to do is give me a name. Unless I have no idea at all who the person is—in which case you'll have to tell me where to find that person."

Then her mood changed, as if just by telling me this much, she'd gotten a load off her shoulders. She sat back on the sofa beside me and spoke in a pleasant, almost chatty, way. "You know, I think you'll pick one of the obvious candidates. A serial killer. A terrorist. A child-molester. A confessed rapist. Somebody already in prison. Khalid Sheikh Mohammed—there's a guy who's proud of his role in 9/11. Pick him and we won't have to go through the spectacle of his trial. There are guys on death row you'd be doing a favor by picking. There are people who are begging for suicide assistance. There's a lady in New Mexico who's put an ad in craigslist asking for somebody to put her out of her misery. 'You will be richly rewarded,' her ad says.'"

Then Maura sort of blurted, "This could even turn out to be a positive experience."

She stopped abruptly, and it was clear that she was startled by what she'd heard herself saying. We both knew she'd gone too far.

"Was Bashar al-Assad a positive experience?" I asked her. I kept my voice low—I wasn't trying to be antagonistic, I just wanted to lead the conversation back to a safe place.

Maura turned her face toward the window. It was dark out there. I thought she wasn't going to answer. But then she turned her eyes back on me, and her face was furious. "Jack, I believe that there are living people who need to be dead!" she said.

"Okay," I said. I wasn't about to argue that point with her.

⌘

I couldn't let it go, couldn't put it out of my mind. Nor could I keep myself from considering candidates. After I got out of the army, I became an enlightened person, but I come from a long line of haters, people singularly gifted at nourishing personal bitterness. To my credit I've mostly stifled that inclination. Such spiritual strength as I have has been directed toward the project of minimizing my hatreds. Even my ex-wife—who seems to have been placed on the planet to infuriate me—will tell you that I have behaved toward her with fairness and civility. Even so, I sometimes wake up in the morning mentally raging at her for moving my son and daughter to the other side of the continent—and this was a dozen years ago. Also when I was ten years old a priest fondled me on a couple of Sunday mornings before early Mass. Were it not for the fact that my priest expired some years ago, I'd have had no difficulty offering his name to Maura. If Shrub were still president, I wouldn't have had to think twice. I was very tempted just to tell her to do the Wyoming guy—there was somebody who had no remorse and who was way overdue for darkness and silence. Besides, it really pissed me off that he somehow managed to get a heart transplant.

But you see, taking on this kind of thinking is like getting on board a train full of beasty demons—I felt gnawed upon and deeply fearful, but the train wouldn't stop, and I couldn't get off. I actually went to the trouble of looking up the ad in craigslist for the lady in New Mexico who wanted a little help getting rid of herself.

In a couple of years I was going to be fifty, I was paying for my kids' education, but they were strangers when I saw them, and we all knew I'd pretty much failed them. My parents were dead, my siblings were right-wingers, I'd accomplished nothing of consequence, my friends were all just acquaintances or former drinking buddies, and I was perfectly suited to living by myself with NPR and the Boston Celtics and micro-brewery beer as my closest companions. I was a day-trader, a lazy one but good enough to make a nice living with a couple of hours of work each morning. But a few years ago, I figured out that I didn't really enjoy spending money. And it had been a couple of decades since I felt anything even similar to love. So now, just by random luck, I had Maura Nelson in my life. Or I had Maura in my life if I was willing to give her a name. If I was willing to become her accomplice.

Maura needed me. I could say that about no one else. Regardless of her motivation for taking up with me, she needed me and only me. Which was to say that she and I both had one chance for a rewarding life, and that chance depended on my agreeing to the bargain she had proposed.

⌘

"Nino."

I was discreet enough not to say even the nickname when she first opened her door to let me in, but the minute she closed it behind me, I spat it out.

She blinked and stared at me. But then she understood and nodded.

We stood in her foyer staring at each other. Evidently we were both comfortable with that way of taking stock of each other.

"Not an admirable choice," she said.

"I can't make an admirable choice," I told her. "I tried being admirable long enough to realize that it wasn't possible for me to do it that way. If I'm going to do this, it has to come out of the truth of me. My worst self," I said. "My worst self is capable of this." My voice probably sounded a little forlorn.

She shook her head, though not necessarily in disapproval.

"Somebody I disagree with," I said. "I disagree with him, and he has great power."

She shrugged. But again it wasn't a gesture of disapproval. It was almost as if she was saying, *Oh you poor fellow, I feel so sorry for you.*

"Well," she murmured, "he can do a lot of harm in the years he has left to live."

Then her mood changed. "Come in," she said. "Let's have some tea." She touched my arm to turn me toward her kitchen. Where I had never been. It was the sunniest, cleanest, tidiest kitchen I'd ever seen. Just looking around improved my mood.

"Oh my, Maura, this is just exactly your kitchen, isn't it?"

She was pleased. She shook a bag of Earl Grey at me, and I nodded. I sat down at the table and enjoyed watching her move from sink to stove top, then reach up to a cabinet to take down a plain tea pot, cups and saucers. No mugs for this occasion. She was wearing a sensible black skirt, sensible clogs, and a sensible grey sweater. She had brushed her hair so that it shone.

"Stop looking at me." She didn't turn to face me when she spoke.

"I was just noticing how profoundly average you look this morning."

We sat at her table with our tea. "Okay to listen to NPR?" she asked, switching on her sound system even before I'd said yes. It was "Morning Edition," with the announcers' voices more familiar to me then than those of my long-dead parents. We listened maybe a half an hour, saying almost nothing to each other. Finally she stood up.

"Nino?" she said, lifting her eyebrows. Her tone was exactly as it might be if she were saying, "Want some more?"

"Nino." My voice was definite.

"Excuse me then," she said. "Fifteen, twenty minutes—I don't think it'll be longer than that." She touched my shoulder as she left the kitchen. In a moment I heard a door close on the other side of her living room.

Then I was alone in Maura's kitchen. I felt fine in that room, and to tell the truth, I didn't really feel like I was alone. The news finished up, and "Fresh Air" was just coming on. Terry Gross always made me feel like the world was still an okay place to live.

POST

For Maura and me, these circumstances of the Supreme Court Justice's death could not have been more seren-dipitous. The narrative was completely persuasive because so many had witnessed what happened. Showing off his mastery, the vain old fellow took a tumble that simulta-neously crushed his skull and broke his neck—a quick, compact story. Out of deference to the singular life of the man—and perhaps subconsciously attempting to restore dignity to a death that had lacked it—no one even brought up the possibility of an autopsy.

Of course Maura had needed to know only approx-imately where her target was. He must have been just taking his first step down the great set of stairs when she pressed the *Enter* command on her computer. My knowledge of what she did was still only approximate and fashioned from ignorance and small knowledge—she'd given me no details, and I'd asked her for none. I can say this, though: When Maura returned to the kitchen from the errand in her study, her appearance had sufficiently changed that I switched off NPR in order to give her my complete attention. As one who has made an informal but lengthy study of the faces of women when they are blush-ing, I can say that there are four reasons why it happens to them—exercise (the least interesting), tipsiness (amusing and sometimes ridiculous), embarrassment (always instructive), and desire (rising or diminishing or full-on active engagement, the latter deeply compelling to me).

"Do you want to turn on the TV news?" she asked me. But since she'd just sat down across from me at her kitchen table, I understood that watching TV was not what she wanted to do. We sat in silence a while. I studied her face, which maintained its rosy pinkness. Though she kept her eyes averted from mine, I felt energy pulsing from her as if she'd ingested a lightning bolt.

"Maura," I said, "I don't think I've ever seen your bedroom, have I?" I kept my voice low, my tone courteous.

Her eyes met mine only a moment. Then she blinked, stood up, and smoothed down her skirt. "This way," she murmured.

⌘

Sex, God bless it, for adults over thirty, is a humbling instructor. Most young men and women sign up for the course with no clue of how ignorant they are, how complicated the subject matter is, and how ineptly they grasp the language spoken by the instructor. Sensei Sex dispenses the good news, the bad, the comical, and the humiliating—but often we students don't get it until we're in our fifties. Maura was thirty-nine and until that morning a virgin. I was forty-five and absurdly more innocent than I ought to have been. I now realize that all those encounters between the sheets when I was a promiscuous young man had taught me almost nothing—about sex, about women, or about myself. What can I say? I was a carnal lout—many a smart young woman told me so as she was making her exit from my bed. I was the guy Paul Simon had in mind when he wrote, "A man hears what he wants to hear and disregards the rest."

I'd like to say that our first coupling was at least a modest success. It did accomplish a desired goal—the breaking of Maura's hymen, which because it had remained intact for so many years had grown sturdy and recalcitrant. So the achievement produced no small amount of pain and blood, which trauma obliterated all desire from both of us. It stunned us into silent action.

The clean-up—stripping the sheets and the mattress pad and tossing them with the towel Maura had laid beneath us into her washing machine—was awkward but necessary. We were both fastidious creatures. Without speaking, we completed the tasks without our clothes. Bloody bedding disturbed us; evidently nudity did not. After we'd put fresh sheets on the bed and while Maura was toweling off from her shower, I finally spoke. "Would you like me to leave now?"

Her face stayed grim, but she shook her head no.

So we lay side by side, staring at the ceiling. Or I stared; Maura may have had her eyes closed. In my peripheral vision I thought I detected a streak of moisture descending from the corner of her eye toward her ear. I couldn't be sure of that and didn't want to disturb her by turning to look. We breathed more or less in unison, lying uncovered and still for I don't know how long. I began to imagine us as frozen male and female samples of our species being shipped through space toward some distant planet. Our bodies and brains would be studied by whatever form of life inhabited the place.

⌘

I have to say this about our nakedness. Earlier in her bedroom, in spite of the high coloring of her neck and face, Maura had undressed in a methodical fashion—almost as if she were in the room by herself. I had watched her and followed her example. Of course I looked. In those moments Maura might have been shy about looking at me, but she seemed untroubled by my gazing at her. Dancer-thin and porcelain-pale—modest but shapely breasts and buttocks and an almost flat abdomen—*astronaut body, pioneer woman's body* were what flashed into my mind. Sex with that body turned out to be problematic; admiration for it was easy.

As to my own carcass, I sometimes told myself that it appeared neither older nor younger than its age. I had a modest paunch and an unappealing stringiness to my arm and leg muscles. I exercised sufficiently and ate with enough restraint to look respectable in my clothes. But naked I was not a sight to stimulate desire in any but the most desperate woman. *He'll do*, would be the best I thought I could expect from Maura. Or maybe, *He won't be so bad.*

Beside her on the bed then, I became aware that Maura was faintly whimpering. Or that's what it sounded like. The noise so faint she might have been some distance away. Something made me understand I should stay still—the way I felt when a wren lit on the windowsill beside where

I sat to drink my coffee in the morning. If I didn't move, the little feathered miracle would stay a while; if I turned my head even slightly it would be forever gone.

When the sound grew a little louder, I decided it might be chuckling. I couldn't tell.

"Jack!" she suddenly bellowed toward the ceiling. Now she was laughing openly and turning toward me. "That was just awful!" she said. "That was just about the worst thing any two people could do together if they were looking for pleasure."

"All right," I said. "All right, Maura." I succeeded in laughing with her, albeit somewhat bitterly. I put my arms around her and pulled her close. She allowed it—seemed even to want it. After a clumsy bit of turning and adjusting and accommodating, she rested her head on my shoulder. Letting our bodies rest together like that must have been comforting because I actually dozed a little, and I think she did, too. And when we woke, we fell into a very cozy chatting, during which she told me of a brother's dying of cancer when she was twelve and he was sixteen. "He was going to be a doctor," she said. "When he got sick, he acted like *he* was one of the doctors treating the illness—and they took him seriously, talked to him like he was one of them. Doctor Nelson they called him. 'What do you think, Doctor Nelson?' one of them would ask him when they made their rounds. The medical staff was as crushed as we were when Ben died."

"Very sad," I murmured when she seemed finished with her telling.

"Yes," she said. "Everything since then has been a lot better than that. Including this," she said quietly.

For a few minutes I entertained the idea of the brother's spirit hovering in that quiet room with us. I wondered what Doctor Nelson would have made of his sister's choosing me as her first sexual partner.

"Will we try it again?" Those words I barely whispered. It was definitely the question of the moment, or maybe of our lives. "Sex, I mean" —and no sooner did I say it than I wished I hadn't. Maura had yet to miss my meaning about anything.

She stayed quiet, though since we were facing each other on the bed, she had to be aware that I was studying her face. She has a high forehead with streaked brown hair usually pulled back from it, somewhat appealingly in disarray at that moment. Also a thin nose with a bit of a ridge, the exact opposite of a button nose—it might have been off-putting except for her lips which were just full enough that I found myself wanting to move my own lips toward them. Yet I knew better. She'd think it invasive, and in that circumstance that's exactly what it would have been. Thinking somebody has pretty lips doesn't give you the right to kiss that person.

"Tomorrow," she said. "I think we can try it again tomorrow."

⌘

We stayed in her bed, chatting drowsily through several hours of that afternoon. Then we meandered into her kitchen for canned soup and crackers. All this while we were as quiet as if we were listening to some pleasant music playing in the next room. Finally, though, I told Maura I thought I should be going.

In the years during which I had lived alone, I had

involuntarily become a loner, and I'm pretty certain she had been that way all her life. If you're that kind of person, then being around someone for several hours can feel unsettling—that's how it had begun to feel to me then, even though I knew that I'd been happy in these hours with Maura. I fully expected her to nod and say okay, see you tomorrow. Instead, she met my eyes and in this touchingly sincere voice asked me if I would come back and stay the night.

"I want us to try having a span of time together—at least twenty-four hours," she said.

Now I was the one to nod. I wouldn't have thought to ask her if I could spend the night, but now that she had invited me, I was eager to do so. So I drove back to my place, gathered up clean clothes, toilet gear, and pajamas—I'd started wearing pajamas when I was married and it had become a habit. That packing up for a sleepover was very agreeable. On the way back to her house, I realized I was sort of inanely happy. It had been so long that I'd forgotten what happiness of any variety feels like.

Maura and I spent some lovely time chatting and nuzzling in bed together before I fell asleep. A little later, of course, I began the snoring that I had warned her about. When I woke myself up with my awful noises, swung myself out of bed and headed for the door of her bedroom, she stirred but didn't complain. "It still counts as staying the night, doesn't it?" I asked her. "Yes," she said. "It counts." But her voice was sleep-groggy, so I couldn't be certain she was okay with my leaving her bed. On the sofa in her living room I quickly went to sleep anyway and experienced a very pleasant dream of my former wife, Vicki, the first I'd had since before we were married. "It counts," the old sweet-faced Vicki told me in her softest voice. She knelt beside me and smiled and caressed my forehead. My dream even included the scent of Vicki's hand lotion. "It counts, Jack, and I'm so happy for you," she whispered.

⌘

In her bathrobe and slippers, Maura woke me with coffee on a tray, with a spoon and a matching sugar bowl and creamer. I sat up in my pajamas. She fetched her own coffee from the kitchen, then sat beside me on the sofa—close, smelling of bath soap and shampoo. Those movements we accomplished with nods, humming sounds, grunts, and single words. No sentences. This part of our morning suited me extremely well. At that time of day my thoughts are reluctant to move toward any declarations.

We'd never previously settled into her living room—always we had walked through it on our way to her kitchen—so this was my first real look at what was, I realized, a cunningly arranged room. The floors were a pale wood—maybe bamboo—polished to the point of almost generating their own light. Her rugs appeared to be a matching set of maroon, blue, and brown East Indian carpets, each one different but connected in a design that suggested, if you lined them up in a certain way, they'd tell a story. Her furniture appeared to be very old mahogany—the wood so deep a brown it was the shade of dark chocolate. There were no mirrors and no paintings, but there were large framed black and white photographs of—I decided as I studied each one from where I sat—people who must all have belonged to the same family: Three women, an old man and two boys, four little girls. Studying one woman who was leaning toward the camera, I became so certain of who she was that I nodded toward the picture and asked, "Your mother?"

Maura took my hand as she stood up, so that I rose, too, and followed her sock-footed across the floor to regard the picture from a foot or so away. I stood close behind her and slightly to the side, with my right hand lightly at her elbow. The woman had Maura's eyes and nose, also Maura's eerie way of slightly widening her eyes and tightening her lips as if she intended to absorb every pixel of what she was seeing. Facing the woman, I felt a little uncomfortable. The photograph was eerily clear, so that details of her face and clothes made her look as if she could speak to us through the glass if she wanted to.

It occurred to me that this woman's expression intended to inform the photographer that she knew him very well. The woman and the photographer were in cahoots in some kind of amusing, unspoken moment. So I decided it had to be Maura with the camera taking her mother's picture. I heard myself make my little *humpf* that usually means, "Okay, I get it." Maura leaned back against me, just enough to make contact with my chest. She said nothing, but she lightly covered my hand at her elbow with her fingers and palm while we stared at the woman a moment longer. Then she reached back with her right hand to take my other hand. "A little slide to the left," she murmured. It didn't seem strange to me to move with her, as if in a dance, step-sliding across the smooth blond floor until we faced the quartet of little girls, each in her own frame. Maura's old bathrobe and worn slippers notwithstanding, I was giddy with standing so close to her.

"Gertrude. Isabelle. Tasha. Annie." Maura tapped the glass of each picture with the nail of her forefinger. "My nieces." She snuggled back against me and pulled my arms around her waist. The four girls examined us with interest. "Eight, ten, eleven, and thirteen," their aunt informed me in a voice as intimate as if our heads were sharing the same pillow.

"What would they think about our murders?" I asked Maura softly. I surprised myself by asking such a question. I hadn't been aware of feeling so edgy. I must have thought this discussion would clear the way for us to move beyond our awful sex of the previous day. I felt the shock of my spoken sentence in her body—a loosening of its strength for just a second, then a slight tightening of her arms on my arms.

"In these pictures, they know it and forgive us," she said finally. "In their lives in the world, they would not believe anyone who told them we did it. Or that *I* did it— they would have no opinion about you." Maura's voice was as steady as if she were making a sworn statement. She kept a firm hold of my arms around her.

We let that information hang in the air. I tried to imagine those cousins out in the world—I thought they must be at least some years older by now. Gertrude. Isabelle. Tasha. Annie must be a young woman, probably in college.

"Now a loop and twirl," Maura said. "Slowly, please."

Though I was no dancer, I learned how to do those moves from Maura's instructive little pushes and pulls. *Let go of her left hand, hold onto her right, step away as she steps back.* We raised our arms to make the bridge underneath which Maura smoothly ducked. Then we stood side by side, each with an arm around the other's waist. "Forward two steps and to the right a couple more," she murmured. "Until we get to Grandpa Durham."

Deliberately as in a dance class we moved our feet, coming to a stop in front of the old man in his overalls and collarless work shirt. His face regarded us with a sneer, his eyes glittered, whether from contempt or affection I couldn't say. I could say, however, that the man must have been quite a piece of work to have as one's grandfather. His chin jutted forward as if inviting someone to hit him. "He knows," Maura said, nodding. "He's the one who taught me how to chop a chicken's head off. When I was six." She squinted, raised her chin toward the big photo, and spoke to it. "Then you had me do a second chicken, didn't you? After I'd done the first and seen how it went. And you watched my face the whole time, didn't you?"

"Grandpa Durham," I said—with some reverence in my voice.

"Yes," Maura replied. "I owe him a lot."

⌘

Knowing that our bodies were capable of moving in accord—and even with something approaching grace—Maura and I commenced teaching ourselves to have acceptable sex. No woman I knew would have so seriously undertaken the task. Or put up with it. But then no woman I knew would have taught me to execute a kind of pas de deux with her in order to view photographs on a wall. At best our sex project was humiliating, though sometimes we were able to see it as a little bit funny.

In those days of our project, we were so absorbed in each other that we ignored the outside world, and the Supreme Court Justice's death seemed like something that had happened long ago. I was at Maura's place so much that we got used to inhabiting the same small space almost all the time. Even so, even in our intimacy, we couldn't seem to align our states of arousal. When Maura finally arrived at the verge of orgasm, I would be tired and drifting along on automatic pilot. "Don't stop!" became the words I dreaded hearing. My sex parts behaved foolishly—suddenly I would come when both of us thought I was nowhere near it. Or else, no matter what lusty shenanigans we resorted to, I wouldn't come at all. And Maura seemed more than a little mystified by her body's unpredictable nature. She, too, came or didn't come erratically but always with muted poise. Whereas I was obvious and imbecilic, she was subtle and understated. I suspected Maura experienced moments of revulsion and hatred for me that she did her best to hide. As for me, several times I almost said aloud that constructing a sexless relationship would be easier than trying to get the hang of successful screwing.

In my most despairing moment, sweating, exhausted, and hovering over her, I did in fact say, "Can't we just be friends?" Maura sadly stared up at me, shook her head, pulled me down against her, softly patted my back, and said, "Oh, bubsy."

Next afternoon—and afternoon seemed to be the time that suited us best for our attempts—she stood before me while I sat on the bed, rested her hands on my shoulders, and peered earnestly into my face. "I think we need to look carefully at each other's *parts*." She checked my face to be certain I know what she meant. "Study them," she said.

"Like playing doctor?" I grinned, but I was completely dreading doing what she had in mind. A young man may feel fine about having his privates examined by a sexual partner, but the thought horrified me. After a certain age, a man figures what he's got down there is probably not so attractive.

"Yes," she said. And grinned, too, but only to indulge me. "That's a good way to think of it."

"Today we have naming of parts," I announced in a stuffy British accent.

She tilted her head at me. "Probably not like that," she said. "Naughty fun," she said. "Think of it like that."

"Okay," I said, but I didn't mean it.

We undressed in our usual way, then lay down on the bed sideways, scooting our bodies in opposite directions to try to face each other's crotches. Just managing the position was a spasm of awkwardness. When we had it more or less right, I willed myself to stay perfectly still. I felt her fingers lightly touching my penis, then lifting it as if to have a better look at my scrotum. The thought made me shudder. Moreover, Maura's upstairs neighbor turned on his radio just loud enough to make an eerie soundtrack for our anatomical investigation. A male voice floated down from the ceiling over us. It was strident but not loud enough to be truly distracting—I couldn't make out the words, though perhaps I could have if I hadn't been so absorbed in what Maura and I were doing.

"Touch me down there," she whispered. "Look. Ask questions. Like, 'What's this?'" Her voice sounded far away, but I felt her fingertip touch the soft little knot of flesh just beneath the underside of my all-too-cooperative glans. I heard some impatience in her voice and didn't respond—mostly because I didn't know what that little part of the penis is called anyway. I did know that it was the liveliest spot on the old gristle. I didn't think about that. I did what I was told and touched Maura's labia. I shifted my arms and shoulders so as to apply the forefingers of each hand to her nether lips. The shifting broke my concentration enough to make me slightly aware of the radio voice above us.

With both fingers I nudged aside the tender little protectors to expose Maura's clitoris. As I faced it, that rosy little nub called to mind an accusatory fingertip pointing at my nose. Guilty of whatever it was it was accusing me of, I held still again. I monitored the messages my penis had begun dispatching to my brain: It approved of what Maura was doing, her light touch. But her clitoris didn't seem to be responding similarly. I couldn't help thinking it had taken a sullen attitude toward me. If anything it seemed to be signaling me to look elsewhere. But I wasn't offended. I felt my penis changing into a cock, rising to the occasion of Maura's playful fingers. The thought occurred to me that the voice from the ceiling was that of an erotic divinity, whispering faintly. *Go ahead, you're about to find out what you need to know.* Maybe this was how God communicated with Adam and Eve in Paradise.

"Interesting," Maura said so softly it was like she didn't want me to hear. Her short pause made me imagine that she had pulled her head back a little distance to be sure she was seeing correctly. "Why, hello there."

While I was gazing at her clitoris, something about

it changed. Or I imagined it changed, because I couldn't be at all certain there was any real difference. I began to think that her clitoris no longer objected to my scrutiny. Something in me understood what was transpiring before my eyes. My head moved closer, my thinning hair touched Maura's thigh. The tip of my tongue ever so tactfully touched Maura's little sweet spot.

She said nothing. But ah, she released such an encouraging sigh she might as well have sent me detailed instructions.

We seemed to know when it was time to shift ourselves back to head-to-head alignment. The sight of her deeply blushing face above me now was still new and thrilling to me. For the next minutes Maura and I were born-again lovers. The voice from the ceiling took on an approving tone. Somehow we had received the knowledge of how we two people could successfully make pleasure. Our mouths and hands and bodies moved with startling exactness. It was sweet but it was also harsh—and maybe at the crucial instant of our pelvises colliding with a grand urgency, it was downright brutal. I felt my whole self fly into Maura at the same time I felt her so completely surrounding me that my body and her body rang in unison like struck cymbals. For that instant we pressed against each other so hard it was as if each of us was trying to become the other.

Because I was holding Maura on top of me with both arms wrapped around her, I felt her begin to shake. At first I thought it was trembling, or maybe weeping, so of course I loosened my arms but left them around her. When she lifted her head, I realized she was actually chuckling.

"All of a sudden," she whispered from deep in her throat, "I understand the word *fuck*."

I chuckled, too. It wasn't ha-ha funny. It was philo-sophical-linguistic funny. And as if to comment on Mau-ra's epiphany, her upstairs neighbor turned up the volume on his radio. Now I could make out the speaker's words even though I really would have preferred not to. ... *tell you who we conservatives are: We love people.*

"Who is that?!" Maura and I asked each other almost in unison. It was a voice we suddenly recognized as one we didn't care for. I loosened my arms, and she pulled away from me. We could hardly stand to touch each other now that we could hear actual words coming to us through the ceiling.

...we see Americans. We see human beings, the voice asserted.

Maura and I stared at each other. "Bloody hell!" I rasped out, and she nodded. "Please don't say his name," she said. "Unless you want to make me sick."

"Dr. Hatemo," I said. "Can I call him that?"

Maura nodded. "Okay," she said. "Good."

We don't see victims. We don't see people we want to ex-ploit. What we see — what we see is potential.

Side by side, we lay still. Of course we listened to the words sifting down to us. We held hands like condemned people listening to a judge describe our punishment. The voice kept talking, with brief interruptions. Hearing it was more and more hateful to us. But then the neighbor upstairs switched it off, and in a moment we heard him in the hallway, locking his door and descending the steps.

Maura and I stayed still a long while. Now the distur-bance I felt streamed from my own mind. "I know what I want is wrong," I finally whispered to Maura.

She turned to me and said, "Thank goodness you want

it, too. I was hoping I wasn't by myself." Her face had that familiar Maura Nelson seriousness that I hadn't seen for several days.

We each stared at the other, holding what we knew—what we alone knew—was like a bowl of fire.

"Do you want me to go in there with you?" I tilted my head toward her study.

She studied my face. Then slowly shook her head. "Thank you," she said softly, "but I can see you don't want to."

"I'm very willing," I said. "I'm with you this time even more than I was before."

Maura smiled, then did a funny thing. She climbed back on top of me and tugged my arms to signal she wanted them the way they were when we came together. We locked into each other again, except this time it was only a little bit sexual—chests and bellies and pelvises as close as we could make them. "I don't mind doing this part by myself," she whispered with her lips right against my ear.

"Okay," I said.

And after a stretch of minutes, she slowly moved away from me, rose from the bed, and put on her bathrobe. Before she left the room, she stared at me and I stared back, my face just as grim as hers. "I'll be back," she said.

"I'm not going anywhere," I told her.

THE THROES

Our vexed death—that was how Maura and I quickly came to think about this one. Assad's was so just and necessary it was as if the stars had required it, and it was executed with such clean precision that it seemed even to us as if the monster died of natural causes. Also the circumstances—of Maura having carried it out alone and in complete secrecy as a test of a method she had discovered by accident—seemed to us extenuating. She and I both treated that death like yes, it had occurred, and yes, we had witnessed it in the making, but her part in it was incidental. Of course the only role I had played was listening to her explain how it had transpired—I knew about it only after the fact.

The Justice's demise allowed us no such moral-ethical slippage. We were responsible—we two. We'd done it. In conversation with Maura I'd even used the m-word. We had, however, with our sex project, constructed a kind of psychological slippage. Which is to say that because we became absorbed in each other and our sexual alignment, Nino had only the flimsiest presence in our thoughts. The nation mourned—and celebrated—grandly, but Maura and I hardly noticed the fuss. To use a word that Maura brought into our conversation, we became temporarily obsessed with fucking. During those days we'd have had to make a conscious effort to feel any remorse over Nino.

So it came to pass that we settled comfortably into more or less ignoring the fact that we'd become murderers. For Maura, the events, both public and personal, had a kind of scientific necessity. She'd deplored the Justice but not with the kind of vehemence that I felt for him. When she'd asked me for a name, I'd given her his. She'd set in motion the forces that produced his death. Then she and I had forged the bond for which she'd unknowingly yearned since she was around twelve years old. And I found the companionship I'd unknowingly needed in order to face my later years.

I confess that I've always been morally and ethically distractible—and perhaps a little too willing to accept my own unacceptable acts. I had a son in Seattle and daughter in San Diego who would testify to my having made little effort to be a father to them. At Christmas and on their birthdays I'd made phone calls. I'd sent them checks. When traveling on the West Coast I'd tried to arrange occasions for visiting them, but when their mother resisted, I didn't fight her. Truth be told, I felt relief. Had I seen my children face to face I'd have felt greater obligation, and seeing me in the flesh, they'd have had all the more reason to despise me for taking so little interest in them and their growing up. I don't know exactly what the term is for the kind of human being I am—maybe something like *only partially realized.* I seem to remember that during our divorce Vicki told her lawyer that I'd somehow never become completely human.

This most recent death, however, was causing Maura and me to rely on each other in reckoning with who we'd become. We had this singular partners-in-crime bond with each other, and we had our hard-won sexual mastery. We really had acquired the carnal knowledge we needed to make sex a force of healing and reconciliation. Our upgraded sex was a way for us to get more truth out of each other. It was also our invisible fortress, a physical solidarity that would be our way of coping with whatever came forth.

The day we understood that we were like-minded in wanting to eradicate the talk show host, I'd stayed in bed and fallen into a bit of a nap while Maura carried out the task in her study. When she slipped back into the bedroom, she did it so quietly I didn't hear her. I woke to the sight of her standing over me, gazing down and smiling in the most affectionate way anyone had ever looked at me. While I watched, she slipped off her bathrobe. Then she made her way under the bedcovers, snuggling up close beside me. "We're really good fuckers, Jack," she said. "You know that, don't you?" I told her that I guessed I did.

⌘

While I was still in the army I'd gotten a call from a broker—probably the newest guy at Goldman Sachs. My uncle had given him my name, and he didn't sneer at my puny little stash of dollars. So I took his advice and bought a couple of telecommunications stocks. I wasn't serious or informed, I just happened to have a thousand bucks sitting in my savings account. And this young man turned out to be some kind of a genius. Bobby Jenkins. Later he told me he surprised even himself. Through the years, a couple of times a week, I'd been giving Bobby a call first thing when he got to office. We didn't even talk about the market all that much, we talked about his poker group and his kids and this little restaurant he bought down in Little Washington, Virginia. "Are we doing anything today, Bobby?" I'd ask him. "Are we making any moves?" and he'd say, "Jack, you want to move some money around, I'll move it for you. How much you want to move?" I'd name a figure, and he'd say, "What I like about you, Jack. You're not greedy. I'll get back to you tomorrow or the next day."

What Bobby and I had in common was what he called the floating factor. Truth be told, the floating factor was a concept I learned from Bobby. Or maybe he just gave me a name for my natural inclination. In any case, he and I both believed that the secret to the whole show was just maintaining a little levitation in our lives.

In the case of Maura, I wasn't exactly clear about the nature of her work, but I did know that she attended long meetings at the Pentagon every other Monday at 1 P.M. I had also noticed that she checked her online account on the first day of each month to see if there had been a deposit, and she once told me, laughing when she said it, that she was on the payroll of the United States Navy. "Somebody probably knows why that's the case," she told me, "but it certainly isn't me."

"Mysterious ways," I said, stifling a smile.

"Mysterious ways," she said, but she was still obviously amused by the fact—or the illusion—that the Navy paid her salary.

⌘

The talk show host was not alone. In the moment of his final heartbeat, a girl was with him in the massive bedroom of his home in Palm Beach. According to the girl, he was reading to her when it happened. She was not reluctant to describe it. She didn't tell it the same way every time, but a point of consistency in her account was how suddenly it had occurred. "He was alive like every day, then all of a sudden he was completely dead," she said. "Poof. Like a magic trick."

"He was reading *Little House on the Prairie*," she told a TV interviewer. "He'd told me I would like that book—he'd already read it to me once. He said it would help me understand important things about Americans. 'A papoose is a little, brown, Indian baby,' he read. He had his big arm around my shoulders, and I remember thinking he had the sweetest voice when he was reading. He stopped because we both liked that sentence. Then he started again— 'They drove a long way through the snowy woods'—and his body twitched, his head kind of snapped back, and his legs kicked a little bit up and down under the covers. The book slipped out of his hands, and he turned his head toward me. I don't think he actually saw me, but he said, 'Oh,' like I'd just told him a secret. Then he was dead. I know how to tell if somebody is dead. I put my fingers to that place on his neck. I felt nothing. I put my palm over his heart and let it stay there a long time. I felt his skin going cool. He was just dead."

In her interviews, when the girl spoke of the talk show host's last moments, she became animated. Once she said she herself was reading the book to him to improve her English. And once she said they were under the bed covers, but another time she said they were lying on top of the covers. She was approximately sixteen, and she went by the name of Kira Gregorevna. She was pretty sure she was born in St. Petersburg, and she thought she had been in the U.S. for three or four years. She was certain she had come to Palm Beach last September to work for the man Maura and I called Dr. Hatemo. The girl said that he planned to adopt her, though she had never seen paperwork to that effect. "He told me that he would do it," she told a social worker who interviewed her in the days that followed the talk show host's death. "Make me his own daughter. I believed him," she said.

The authorities were, by turns, intrigued and baffled by the girl. She had no documents. She didn't know who or where her parents were. She said she came to the U.S. with "some men." She said she worked in Atlantic City and Philadelphia for more than a year, though she didn't remember any details of her employers. The authorities believed she was withholding many details of her time in Atlantic City and Philadelphia, though they had not been able to turn up anything about that part of her history. Nor had they discovered anything about her Russian childhood. She was highly sophisticated in terms of clothes, food, TV, movies, and computers. However, she read English at the level of a second grader and Russian not at all. Or she said she didn't know how to read any Russian at all, and she remembered only a few phrases of the spoken language. Though her stories were various and conflicting, she always gave the appearance of speaking as frankly and truthfully as she could. "I want to help, but my memory is very bad," she said. She had a kind of innocent energy about her, though when one saw her on TV, one couldn't help thinking maybe her girlish affect was a persona she had constructed.

Kira Gregorevna said that Dr. Hatemo was like a father to her. She said that every week he put money into a savings account for her so that she could go to college. Bank records confirmed what she said. Rumor had it there was a savings account in her name at a Palm Beach branch of Bank of America with a balance of a little more than $400,000 in it. The girl kept track of it online, and she had declined to reveal the password for that account to the authorities. She said that Dr. Hatemo was very kind to her. She said that he never attempted to have sex with her, though she did have sex with some other American men in Philadelphia. She said she needed money, and that was her only way of getting it. "Anyone not a fool would have done what I did," she said.

The authorities surmised that Kira Gregorevna was a victim of international sex trafficking and that she probably came to be in the company of Dr. Hatemo by way of a financial transaction. Which is to say that she probably made her way to this country as a commodity. Men paid other men for her. Which is to say that it's likely that Dr. Hatemo purchased her, too. Authorities say they have found no evidence that that was the case. They say there is almost never a paper trail for such transactions. They say that when they asked Kira if she was Dr. Hatemo's slave, she laughed in their faces. "I think he was *my* slave," she said. By way of explanation, she said that he gave her whatever she asked for and did whatever she asked of him.

Kira Gregorevna had a lawyer who represented her, a young woman who believed that the girl needed little oversight or advice. "Wise beyond her years," the lawyer said. Helen Navarro, an associate in the firm that had represented the talk show host for many years, had managed to appoint herself as the girl's guardian. Helen Navarro had successfully argued that because there were no official documents pertaining to the girl anywhere in the world and because no one could prove she had lived anywhere but here, Kira Gregorevna was a de facto citizen of the U.S. Helen Navarro said that the girl obviously had the right to live wherever she wished in this country. She argued that until Dr. Hatemo's estate was settled, the girl had the right to continue living in his home. Staff members of Dr. Hatemo's household had stepped forward to say that they were accustomed to thinking of Miss Kira as family—"his closest kin" was the phrase they used to speak of her—and they were very comfortable with her staying in the home. The authorities had been treating both Helen Navarro and Kira Gregorevna with notable respect.

All of the above information had unfolded in various manifestations of the national media. What was troublesome to Maura and me about the story of Kira Gregorevna was that every variation of her account of the death of the talk show host suggested the possibility of something other than natural causes. Especially the suddenness of it. Nothing in the talk show host's medical history explained the speed of his death.

CNN's Stella Grace was on top of this story from the beginning. Ms. Grace herself interviewed the girl on three different occasions and took the position that Kira Gregorevna herself was a victim who might have been a pawn in a plot against the talk show host. "We all know there are hundreds of people out there who have wanted to shut him down for years," Ms. Grace stated more than once on her show. Almost every evening she called for Attorney General Holder to investigate the matter. "If this great American hero had been a Black liberal, the feds would have been all over this case," Ms. Grace said. No one stepped forward to contradict her. Kira Gregorevna did not speak to these political matters, though she did agree with Stella Grace that Dr. Hatemo's death was peculiar. "It freaked me out, that's for sure," she told Stella Grace on camera, her voice tinkly, adolescent, and bemused. CNN still played that clip at least once every twenty-four hours. On TV Kira Gregorevna had the look and body language of a Rollins College first-year.

⌘

So this vexed death—and all news of it—had taken hold of Maura's and my attention as the two previous deaths never had. This one threatened to divide us. My view was, after my initial panic, that there was no possibility that Maura and I would be discovered to have any connection with what happened to the talk show host. Maybe the authorities could prove that the man didn't die of natural causes, but I couldn't imagine how they could go further than that. Neither Maura nor I had had any contact whatsoever with the talk show host. So I saw our mission to be only one of setting the experience behind us. "We can let it go," I said to Maura several times. "We can act as if we had nothing to do with it until that's what it feels like to us. That's what we did with Nino, and look how happy we were in those days."

Maura didn't actually disagree with me, but she

couldn't let go of it. I wasn't sure she was trying to. "That girl," she said in her quiet-and-serious voice. "That girl actually watched him die right in front of her eyes. She makes me want to feel it as if I watched it happen, too. He was so despicable I knew he needed to be dead, but I didn't witness it. Doesn't it mean something to you, Jack—that she saw it? That she actually saw what we made happen?"

"You never imagined how it would look?" I asked her.

"Did you?" she responded.

"I didn't," I told her. "But I'm not the one… "

"The one who, Jack?" Now she raised her voice, and her face went a little hard in a way I hadn't seen before. "Are we not in this together? Have you been thinking all these weeks that you are merely an accessory? Is that where we are? I'm the killer, and you're just the helper?"

A shadow flew through my mind—if I angered Maura deeply enough, what might she do? I didn't look away from her face, but I actually felt my thoughts skittering away from that question.

Every relationship I'd ever been in had had a moment like that—albeit with notably lower stakes—where one had a choice to speak the truth that was sure to cause damage or to tell the lie that might not be convincing but would enable the couple to continue. For example, "Do you like this perfume?" "Do you think I spoke too aggressively at the Stinsons' party last night?" "Do you like it when I do this to you?" "How do I look in this dress?" "Where have you been?" If a truthful answer was possible, then no problem, but if a lie seemed a kinder choice, then—Ah well, then the continuing was always problematic. The man and the woman have to function like a couple in a three-legged race—they can do it, and they can even get used to it. Sometimes they can function that way so long they fool themselves into thinking everything is back to normal.

"Until you just now said it, I wasn't aware that that was how I was thinking. But you're right. I'm very sorry to admit it." My voice was shaking, whether from fear or guilt I couldn't say, but I also couldn't help feeling proud of myself for stepping into the difficulty. "I'm not sure I would even call it thinking, but if that's what it is, then yes, what it feels like to me is that you're leading and I'm following."

Maura met my eyes for only a moment longer. Then she glanced away. Her face still looked stony, as if in the next moment she was going to say, "Get out." I was already considering the logistics of moving my things out of her apartment. God help me, I was even imagining Maura walking slowly into her study as I left her apartment after our final goodbye.

Then she turned a softer face to me—it was not a smile or a grin, but it was an okay look. I knew she meant it, she was coming around to forgiving me, and I knew we'd be all right for at least a while. "I've enabled you to do that," she said. "I shouldn't have," she said.

"Maybe we won't ever do anybody else," I told her. "Then it won't matter," I said.

We were quiet, and even though we kept on staring at each other, it felt like we had finished the hard part, and we were back to the man and woman, the double mind that turns a dull life into an exciting one. Then Maura turned her head down and shaded her eyes with her hand. "I wish I could believe that," she said. "But I'll bet you know as well as I do. We'll do it again."

"We don't have to," I said much too quickly. The words sounded unpleasantly shrill, even to my ears.

⌘

"I have to see her. I have to talk to her."

"Bad idea," I said. "Unless you want to invite every law-enforcement agency with an interest in this case to send some people to knock on our door."

"There must be a way to do it," Maura said. "We're smart people."

"Not that smart," I said.

⌘

I was slow coming to understand this: Once Maura gave me the knowledge of what she was doing, she bestowed upon me the power to change her life in ways she wouldn't want. I could have had her put in prison. Which I knew she would hate. And I gave some thought to that: imagined myself in court, testifying against her. I even imagined Maura behind bars, powerless. But I didn't have the ability that she had—to murder me without leaving a clue that she'd done it. So it wasn't the same for me. My thoughts about betraying her were frivolous, whereas I thought her consideration of editing me out of the picture would necessarily be serious. She had the power. She either had to use it, or not. Her need for me was maybe 7 percent sexual and 93 percent as her companion in crime. Which was to say that I couldn't really blame her for seeing me as non-essential. This never showed in her face, her words or her manner, but every single day Maura must have had to make a decision about whether or not to allow me to continue with my life.

⌘

In this time of estrangement, I found myself sustained by my—I didn't know what to call it—appreciation, affection, admiration, whatever—for the ways of Maura's body. This was more about desire in the abstract than it was about sex. I'm talking about how she walked across a room, sat down cross-legged in an easy chair, held her back straight and stared out a window for some minutes. It was oddly impersonal, as if I'd become the roommate of Degas's "Little Dancer." The precise and elegant motions of her hands as she boiled water for tea, of her fingers and how she managed the tea pot, the small canister for the loose tea, the mug, her setting aside of the canister and her transporting the mug to her chair. It was as if I had acquired a camera's devotion to a subject. I found myself dissolved in observing her gathering up her loose hair with both hands behind her head, squeezing it into a tight bundle, then twisting it up and arranging it into a knot with a little plume of strands extending upward and slightly to the side. Even her hair had a kind of modest insouciance. What she executed as unconsciously as scratching her ear produced what I couldn't help seeing as a work of art.

This mode of "seeing" generated a good deal of confusion in me. Sometimes I wanted to go quickly to her, embrace her and whisper in her ear, "Can we please just get in bed right now?" More often the sight of her pulled me along like a mild version of gravity. I yearned to be her shadow, to be as near her as possible but also to remain invisible, unobtrusive. Mostly I wanted to watch without her knowing. I believed that she was very slightly aware of my watching and I speculated that if she thought about it at all, she didn't mind. I even imagined that she liked it, that maybe all these years of living alone she'd wanted someone to gaze at her as I did.

Occasionally there would be a significant treasure in my visual experience of her. There was a chair at a window in her living room where Maura often arranged herself backwards so as to look out the window at the chickadees and titmice in the limbs of the ash tree out there. Once I stepped into the living room to see her holding the back of the chair with both hands, with one knee in the chair's seat and with the opposite leg extended upward toward the ceiling. It seemed to me a nearly impossible yoga position. She wore the old t-shirt and gym shorts she enjoyed for days when she worked at home, and yet the pose startled me as if I'd found her standing naked in a stream of sunlight. Her back was to me, and I was in my sock feet and had made no noise, and so I didn't think she knew I was there. She held the position for maybe a couple of minutes, long enough for me to speculate about what might have called it up in the first place. A yoga pose? A stretching exercise? A peculiar form of meditation? After a moment I felt her realize my presence in the doorway; in the next moment she tipped herself back to a standing position facing the chair. She looked over her shoulder at me and said matter-of-factly, "Yellow warbler."

I thought a moment and then said, "Yellow warbler. Yes, of course."

That vision of her—one slim leg sending up her foot to point at the ceiling—permanently installed itself in my mind. And even if she made up that explanation for what she was doing, I liked to think that it was the sight of a yellow warbler that called forth her body's response.

We went on with our day.

⌘

Maybe most of all what the watching did was make me want to move with her, as we did the day we looked at the photographs on the wall. Sometimes her facial expression actually invited me to take up that dance with her in the kitchen as we were fixing drinks. Or after dinner clearing the table, we would find ourselves in a peculiar accord of matched steps, matched movements of our heads, arms, and torsos. It was an improvised choreography that seemed to wait quietly for us to pick it up—and then to let it go. I was all the more pleased by our not discussing it. It was calming—that way our bodies sometimes spontaneously agreed to move in unison.

That Maura was brilliant—or that I believed she was brilliant—informed my passion for observing her. If I had thought she was simple-minded or uneducated or shallow, I'd have found the look of her less compelling. That's what had happened with Vicki and me—I'd come to understand that there was nothing about my wife's thinking that interested me. Therefore I stopped being able to see her obvious beauty. As I paid her less and less attention she seemed to work at making herself more beautiful. Friends who knew us occasionally let it slip that they thought I was a fool for letting her go, a woman who turned heads even after she had reached middle age and given birth to two children. I thought I was a fool, too, but what can

I say?—I had needed her to speak to me in a way that I couldn't disregard. I'd needed her to say or do something that knocked me back. I like to think I was ready to receive evidence of her being someone I should hold in higher regard. In my opinion I gave her more than enough time to say the words that would demand my respect. I never spoke of this to anyone because I was ashamed of how I felt about Vicki. It was beyond me to correct my response to her. It always felt like my failure, my fault, my bad.

When I thought like this—when I did the cost accounting of my marriage to Vicki—I had to remind myself that Maura and I rarely had intellectual conversations. We talked only indirectly about science or art or politics. We talked about what came to mind, which is to say that we mostly talked about people. Family. Acquaintances. Writers. Characters in books or in the movies or plays. Somebody in the news. We both liked animals a lot, and our conversations about birds and whales and coyotes were usually playful. We knew we were childish to be the way we were. We once had an ongoing episodic discussion about Jennifer Lawrence, the very young film star, currently on the cover of *Vanity Fair* with a caption asserting that she was "the World's Most Desirable Woman." We agreed that the caption was ridiculous, that the article and the pictures that accompanied it were a besmirching of the young woman's talent, and that this was what we hated about America. Or about the privileged class of people throughout the world.

"To which of course we belong," Maura said to me over wine after dinner. When I agreed with her, her eyes flashed. "But you do desire her, don't you?" she said. Her voice made it clear she wasn't really asking a question.

"In the abstract," I said, "I do. I confess that there are a couple of scenes in the film *Silver Lining Playbook* that if I'd had the power to step into, I'd have tried to get her in bed with me."

"Ha!" said Maura. "Ha" was a syllable she and I couldn't do without. It meant you're right, you're wrong, you're very funny or smart or stupid or whatever. It was always a bemused thing to say—simultaneously challenging and sociable.

"On the other hand," I went on, "in *Winter's Bone*, there was never a moment when I wanted to be in bed with her. In fact, in that movie, all I wanted was for her to be safe in her own bed by herself with nothing to worry about. If I'd accidentally found myself in bed with that kid, I'd have gone straight to the sheriff and asked him to put me in jail."

"You're such a boy scout," Maura said.

"About as much as you are a girl scout," I said. Then I said—because I suddenly knew it was true— "You desire her, too. Don't you."

She bowed her head. Stayed silent. Then gave me a sheepish grin. "In the abstract," she barely murmured.

We both appreciated those little checkmate points in our conversations. We came to them only because we were so like-minded. Even after our wine glasses needed refilling we lingered at the table with contented faces turned to each other.

⌘

"Philo T. Farnsworth," she said. "You ever hear of him?"

This was on a rainy afternoon when I was bored and

loosey-goosey with being trapped in the apartment all day. In my mood, I had taken to pestering Maura about how her knowledge came to her. I had been in and out of her study for most of the day. So I was in there, and we were both aware that I was just trying to get her attention, which tended to wander away from me and stay away for longer periods of time than I liked. I had succeeded in getting her irked at me, but I hadn't yet received anything like an answer from her. So maybe now that she had spoken up, maybe things were about to change.

"You're making something up," I said. "That's a made-up name."

"Google him," she told me, keeping her back turned. "His first name is spelled P-h-i-l-o. His last name is spelled just like it sounds."

When I returned to the living room to look up Farnsworth, I found plenty of information. This was the guy who more or less invented television, but he did a lot of other things, too. While I was educating myself on this weirdo genius, I started wondering if maybe Maura hadn't just sent me off on an errand that would keep me out of her study for a little while. But if that was her goal, she nevertheless had an eerie sense of the right person to send me off to research. It wasn't so much that he invented television as that he just got an idea about how television might be possible.

I stepped back into her study, making sure to generate a little noise. Even so, Maura kept her back turned and her head unmoving as she continued tapping away at her keyboard. It occurred to me that the steady cadence of her fingers in her work "for the U.S. Navy" lacked the urgency of the be-bop clattering I heard those same fingers generating in our assassination projects.

"Philo Farnsworth was a child prodigy," I announced. "Grew up in a log cabin. Not a lot of education. Figured out how to do television."

Maura's keyboard tapping neither slowed nor speeded up, but she did nod her head ever so slightly. And in a moment, when she seemed to have reached a stopping place, she swiveled her chair around to face me. "And did you read about how he figured out television?" she asked. Maura would have made a pretty good schoolteacher if she'd taken that path rather than the one she did take.

"Maybe I skimmed that part," I said. "Didn't know there was going to be a quiz."

At least the shadow of a grin flickered across her face. "Fourteen years old, Philo was walking behind a team of horses plowing his family's potato field. He turned around and saw the parallel lines he and his horses had made with their plodding back-and-forth over the field. It struck him that the lines they'd carved so painstakingly in the dirt could be the way to break down an image so that it could be reproduced on a screen. His mind leaped from what was right in front of his eyes." Maura kept her eyes on mine. "Leaped to something way beyond what he was looking at."

"All right," I said. I stood waiting for more, but more was not forthcoming.

"And in your case?" I murmured.

She was quiet for a long moment. I couldn't tell if she was trying to remember or trying to decide if she really wanted to tell me.

"A day of crazy weather," she finally said. "It was a Monday, because the night before, I'd watched a piece on *Sixty Minutes* about the military guys out in Nevada who actually do the calculations and push the buttons for the drone strikes. I'd gotten caught in a thunderstorm in that big parking lot at Taft's Corners, when all of a sudden the heavy rain had turned into hail, not really big hail but small pellets—about the size of a pencil erasers—that clattered on my umbrella. And the week before I'd read a *Smithsonian* article on laser technology in hospitals." She stared intently at me.

"And?"

She shook her head. "And my mind did what Farnsworth's mind must have done, felt a connection and crunched out a calculation," she said. "One minute I didn't know anything. Not a clue. Next minute there it was in my head, the whole shebang." She released a snorty little laugh that I was pretty certain was a result of having said *shebang* aloud. She must have had that word stored up in her mind from the first minutes of understanding what the hail pellets were telling her. "Like a lesson in advanced physics that I'd learned in my sleep," she said.

I grinned at her. I liked where this story was going. "Can you say more?" I asked.

She stared at my face a good thirty seconds, as if trying to decide if I was worthy of knowing the secret. "Yes," she finally said. Then she gave another sigh, this one to inform me that she had made her decision and that we had come to the end. "But I won't. And you should be very grateful to me that I'm not going any further than that."

That sigh and her tone of voice really irked me. "I'll work on that," I said. "The gratitude," I said, just so she would know that it didn't sit so lightly with me. I turned and left her study, but I wasn't upset enough to slam the door behind me. I was just mad enough to make sure I closed it without making a sound.

⌘

I was reading the *Times* on my tablet. Maura had been in her study, but almost from the instant she opened the door, I knew something was up with her. She stood over me, hands on her hips, her face very serious. "Nan Salter," she said. Salter was a TV commentator so extreme that I was a little shocked at Maura for saying her name—and perhaps proposing her as someone we should consider transitioning.

That I was taken aback was fine with both of us. It was also fine for me to take my time considering what she was proposing. I studied her face. With Maura what seemed to be up might not in fact have been what was up.

"No," I said.

"And?" she said.

"Nan Salter is not serious," I said. "Not worthy of what we would be...." I had to find the right phrase here. "Not worthy of what we would be bestowing upon her."

Maura smirked. "Magna Cum Laude from Cornell. University of Michigan Law School. Editor of their law review. What do you mean, 'not worthy'?"

Now she was studying me. I suspected her of something, I wasn't sure what.

"The harm she does is small. And a little bit laughable," I said. Then I sort of got what was going on in Maura's mind. She was trying to define for both of us what we were doing. The thought that had occurred to her was if we took out the talk show host, why not somebody similar? She needed me to validate a conclusion she'd probably already reached.

"Nan Salter might be worse than the radio guy," she said. "She's on TV. She reaches people. Just like he did, she creates, nourishes, and manipulates hate. Just like him, she knows better. Just like him, she does it for money."

I had to look away from Maura. There was something I needed to say, but I couldn't quite find the words for it. "She's low on my list," I said. "And I'm certain she's low on yours."

"I don't have a list," she said.

"I don't either," I said, "but we could each come up with one in about thirty seconds."

She turned her back to me and walked over to the window where maybe there would be cardinals or chipping sparrows to cheer her up. Maybe this was really what her trouble was. She had the blues.

"I kind of hate us," she said.

"Well," I said. I thought a while in silence. "Then maybe Nan Salter is the reason we can stop here. Without going any further. Whenever another candidate presents him- or herself to us, we can turn on the TV or look for a picture of Nan Salter. Whenever we see her face, it will remind us why we stopped."

Maura stood at the window. Gave me her back to study. Which was fine with me. She had on a hip-hugging black skirt that would be immodest if she weren't wearing tights with it. Her shoulders in her royal blue blouse summoned me to step up quietly behind her to massage the tendons extending down from her neck. I knew better, though. She was going through something. And she was trying to move me through it along with her. Even if I didn't really understand.

"No," she said finally. "Nan Salter can't stop us. But that's the problem, isn't it?"

"That nobody can stop us?" I didn't wait for her to answer. "You know what the answer is to this question you're hammering yourself with."

"Tell me," she said.

"Either we'll stop ourselves, or we'll keep on doing what we do."

"That answer is intolerable!" she spat out. She didn't turn to let me see her face, but I couldn't remember her ever sounding so angry before.

"Yes," I said. "Yes, it is. Intolerable." When I said that word, I realized something—or I thought I realized it. This was the name of the place where Maura was right then—*intolerable*. She and I couldn't help believing that certain awful people needed to be dead, and because we could do it without getting caught, we made them dead. But then Maura loathed herself for doing it. I was with her in this regard, but it didn't bother me as much as it did her. She was struggling to find a way out. And I knew I'd better do what I could to help her find it.

We stayed quiet for a couple of minutes, Maura gazing out the window, me sitting with my tablet in my lap. Studying her back, which was still and tense.

After a while she turned toward me, her expression washed out, more than a little grim. "I'm going to try to see her, you know."

I sighed. "This is not Nan Salter you're talking about." I had a bad feeling.

She didn't reply, and of course I didn't want her to. "You have a plan?" I asked.

I knew the answer to this question, but Maura honored me by nodding slightly.

"You've done some research of course."

She nodded again.

I studied her, though I couldn't tell much more from her face other than that she was hurting. "Am I in your plan?" I asked.

Before she answered, there was just enough of a pause to generate a little disturbance in my mind. "Only if you want to be," she said very softly.

"You know I do," I said.

"I know you think it's a bad idea to contact her," she said.

I shook my head. "Doesn't matter," I said. "Above everything else I trust you. That's how we got here. It's how we have to try to get out. That's what I know right now."

While I watched her, her face relaxed. Which pleased me a lot. I grinned at her. "Do you think we'll like her?" I asked.

Maura appreciated the question, the move away from our gloom. She managed a grin of her own and stepped forward, reached down to pull me up to a standing position. "Yes," she said. "We are probably going to like her. And if we don't like her, then we can enjoy hating her together. Come with me," she said.

I knew where she was leading me. I was just as eager to get there as she was.

AT THE BEACH

Kira Gregorevna sat on a bench by the ocean near the tiny public section of Palm Beach Shores. Every day, no matter what, for an hour or two in the late afternoon, alone. She wore sunglasses and a scarf, no make-up, loose-fitting cotton slacks, old-style sandals, and a baggy long-sleeved t-shirt. Evidently she wore a good deal of sunscreen because the skin of her face was pale as an invalid's. She resembled a middle-aged woman who was ill. Someone who was recovering from chemotherapy—or maybe progressing in the other direction. A lady who had decided to spend her last days near the ocean, sitting quietly, gazing toward the horizon. This person bore almost no resemblance to the Kira Gregorevna who had appeared on the Stella Grace show.

I didn't know the details of how Maura came to possess such information. I didn't ask her, but when she described the girl's ritual for me, I raised my eyebrows. "I paid for it," she said. She went on to say that her source assured her that the girl managed to leave Dr. Hatemo's estate without being observed and that she was not under surveillance during this time she spent at the beach. When I raised my eyebrows again, Maura said, "Other than by my source." She met my eyes, shrugged, looked away.

So we both knew that already we had most likely been compromised. A couple of weeks ago, I had argued against going any further with Maura's plan. At that moment, sitting across from each other at her kitchen table, I came into possession of three pieces of knowledge. 1) Maura was not entirely brilliant—or her brilliance evidently didn't apply to ordinary human relationships. 2) Going further with her plan to make contact with Kira Gregorevna was almost certain to provoke the FBI to take an interest in us. 3) Even so, I was "all in," as they say in poker. I was surprised at how far my feelings had evolved. Even if I was just a follower, I could see that I was more committed to Maura than I ever had been to my former wife.

Because any one of those revelations could be devastating for me, I took some pride in registering them without even blinking. Maura and I were dawdling over the last of the coffee. She had put herself in a trance by studying something on her tablet over on the kitchen counter, which gave me license to study her. She was in her bathrobe, and she hadn't showered or fixed her hair as she ordinarily would have done before she even sat down there with me. So I knew she hadn't slept well. I suspected her of giving me some time while we sat there to process what she had revealed. By inquiring about the girl, she'd made it known that we had an interest in the girl. People who sell information look for ways to maximize their profits, and Maura's informant certainly knew that the authorities would like to know about anyone who asked questions about Kira Gregorevna. Maura might not have been completely brilliant about private detectives, but when it came to reading my mind she was way ahead of anybody I'd ever known. I suspected her of knowing my thoughts before they even arrived in my brain. And with what we were about to do, I suspected both of us of being fools.

"Did you book the flight?" I asked her.

She nodded but didn't meet my eyes.

"Two tickets?"

This time she did meet my eyes, and there was a flicker in her glance that I translated to mean, "Thank you."

⌘

That past month we'd both given our jobs very little attention. Maura's boss had called her in to tell her that she'd built up a lot of credibility with her contributions the past several years, that he thought everyone went through rocky times, that if she had to take a little time off she shouldn't worry, because he wasn't worried about her, but that if she ever needed to talk with somebody about any little problems or issues, he was there for her. Though I don't answer to anyone with my day trading, I did get an email from my contact in New York asking me if I was okay, because according to his records, I was now losing money at about the same pace that I ordinarily made money. My retirement portfolio was doing just fine, and in my line of work, losing money, if it doesn't go on too long, just means paying lower taxes. So both Maura and I had way too much slippage in our places of employment to cause us to worry. The thought occurred to me that if we were really pressed to make a living, we might be less inclined to do what we did. And I thought that a trip to Florida might bring us a fresh perspective to help us move through our time of difficulty. The other day in conversation with Maura I came up with a word for it when I said, "Our conundrum is like a bad roommate—a nasty-tempered slob who won't move out."

She stopped taking glasses and plates out of the dishwasher, gave me a look, and asked, "What do you mean?"

"We're driven to do what makes us feel awful," I said.

"Our life makes us hate our life," she said. "Conundrum. Good word," she said and went back to the dishes and plates.

"Yes," I said, very proud of myself.

⌘

We sat down on either side of the lady in sunglasses and a scarf. Maura introduced herself and me as writers working on a story about "the real people" of Palm Beach. *This is very crude,* I told myself, while Kira Gregorevna carefully scrutinized Maura. *She's never going to believe this,* I told myself. I expected the girl to give me a similar inspection, but she didn't even turn my way. "You're from New York?" she asked Maura. And it was her voice that gave her away as being a youngster. In that sunlight her face looked as flat and washed out as that of a woman who'd lived hard for some years.

"We hope to sell our story to *New York Magazine,*" Maura said brightly. "Or maybe the *Times* Magazine. We're freelancers."

"You have a recording machine?" the girl asked.

"I do," Maura told her. Which was a surprise to me. I was even further surprised when she reached into her straw purse and pulled out a recorder about the size of a cell phone. I had no idea she owned such a device. I began to think that I had underestimated Maura, that maybe she'd understood exactly how we should approach Kira Gregorevna—directly and with a story that was so obviously false the girl would believe it. Maybe if we'd been cunning, the girl would have stood up and walked away from us. During this exchange between them, the girl still had not glanced at me. Though her face wasn't visible to me then, I was pretty sure she was beaming at Maura.

"May I see it please?"

When Maura placed the recorder in the girl's hand, I felt a small uptick in my anxiety. Maybe the device would persuade Kira Gregorevna that Maura and I were imposters. She examined it admiringly. "So compact," she said, weighing it in her open palm. Then she pointed a clear-polished fingernail to its red switch. "To turn it on?" she asked.

Maura nodded.

With a flourish Kira Gregorevna pressed the switch and smiled, first at Maura and then (at last!) at me, lifted the little box with the fingers of both her hands up to within a few inches of her mouth, cleared her throat, and said, "What would you like to know?"

I was startled, and I was sure Maura was, too, but to her credit, surprise wasn't visible in her facial expression. "Tell us how you got here," Maura said, her voice animated and encouraging. "Tell us who you are and how you came to be sitting here on this bench."

"Well," began Kira Gregorevna, again glancing first at Maura and then at me. "How much time do you have?"

⌘

Kira said that she came to the U.S. from Russia when she was quite young. She remembered only a few details about the city of Bronnitsy—her grandmother who had no teeth, a lake with a bridge so you could walk across it, a café with people smoking. There was a river, too—her cousins told her about it—but she wasn't sure she ever saw it herself. "That's it for Bronnitsy and me," she said, chuckling. "A little city. Means nothing to me. An old dream. Very fuzzy."

Because she was a clever girl her cousins brought her to Philadelphia, where she helped with their business for many months. When she was old enough, she traveled with her cousins to work in Atlantic City. "That's where I met a famous man and came here to work for him," she said. Her face became animated as she spoke about him. "If you don't mind, I won't tell you that man's name. You would know him, but he's dead now. Which makes me very sad. I want to tell you about him, but I don't want to talk about how famous he was. Around me it made no difference anyway. He was the kindest person I ever knew, and a great teacher. I learned from him.

"Three weeks ago yesterday he was teaching me to drive. Time for you to learn, he said. That surprised me, but I was ready. He owned I don't know how many cars. Americans love cars, he told me. He said he had more cars than anybody, and not a one of them cheap. He said cheap cars were fine for Russians and Japanese, not Americans. He thought it would be better for me to learn to drive in a big car. These things almost drive themselves, he told me. This was a Lincoln Navigator he chose for me to learn how to drive—big as a bus. Sitting behind its steering wheel, I felt very small. He pointed to the pedals at my feet and told me their names, the brake and the accelerator; he thought I would know what they were for. So the Navigator drove itself into the side of another car in his driveway. A shiny grey Mercedes. Why didn't it stop?! I shouted at him. I smacked the steering wheel with both my hands. Oh, baby, my boss said, I love you. The Navigator with us in it was still rocking while he was talking. Thirty seconds behind the wheel you have a $50,000 accident. He laughed and laughed. You're my kind of gal, he said.

"So I asked him, what is a *gal*. I'd never heard the word. In this country, he said, a gal is what you want to be. Everybody loves a gal, he said. You're not one yet, but I'll help you learn. We were still sitting in the car then, staring at the poor Mercedes I'd just smashed. My boss had turned off the Navigator's ignition, and we were just sitting there. You know what?, he said. He was still laughing. I think you need to learn how to smoke a cigar. That's maybe the first step you need to take on the way to becoming a gal. So he took a new cigar out of his shirt pocket, unwrapped the cellophane, and asked me to put it in my mouth. Not in the front, he said, but in the side, so I could hold it with my jaw teeth. I'd just wrecked two of his cars, I wasn't going to say no. He held a lighter for me and told me to take a puff. Don't inhale, he said. Just take a puff then let it slowly out of your mouth. If you take a liking to these things, I'll show you how to blow smoke rings. I hated the cigar, and he could see that. But I liked it that while we sat in his broken car, he tried to teach me to smoke cigars. He was funny in a way that made me know he liked me."

Kira told us she'd seen the famous man get mad a few times. She'd seen him curse the Cuban worker who tended

his rose garden. He fired that worker because the man refused to water the roses the way he was supposed to. Kira
thought then maybe she should be afraid of her boss. "He
was no giant, but he was a big enough man to hurt me if he
wanted to," she said. "When I saw him with the gardener
that day, I knew it was easy for him to get mad. He was
loud and mean. I even thought he liked being mad. But
that day in the car I decided he probably would not get
mad at me—unless I stole from him or tried to hurt him.

"I've talked about this to nobody, so I'm going to trust
you to believe what I'm about to tell you. My job wasn't
what you think. If you write the story and don't tell the
truth, I will come looking for you. I used to hear my boss
say that to people on the phone, then he would go ha ha
after he said it. I decided he meant it as a joke that would
scare them a little bit. So that's what I'm saying to you—if
your story twists my words or makes me look like a bad
person, I will come looking for you."

Kira told us that the famous man brought her into his
home in this city, and he told her she would never have to
do anything bad again. He knew about the things she'd
had to do in Philadelphia and Atlantic City. He told her
that in his home she could put all those things behind
her and be a new person. "He made this gesture around
us when he said that about his home—like his beautiful
house would turn me into a good person. So you want
to know what it means for me to be sitting here on this
bench? It means I have a new life. It means that when I
sit here I know I'm an American. I look out there, and I
know I came here from a place that's so far away across
that water it feels like a story in a book. A place where
people beat me, and I almost starved to death. Every day

that I sit here I know it again. I'm here and not there. Even if he's dead now my boss gave me this."

Because Kira had gotten teary talking about what her boss did for her, we just sat beside her quietly, all three of us gazing out over the water. After a while she took a deep breath and began speaking again without our having to question her.

"Okay, my job. I'll try to tell you. The man I worked for, my boss, he said I should call him that when I speak about him to people who don't know. I am your boss, he liked to tell me. I know it was his way to remind me how lucky I was. So my boss told me the story of Elvis Presley. He said Elvis Presley was one of the greatest Americans. After Ronald Reagan, he said, Elvis might have been the greatest. He said Elvis wrote a letter to President Nixon to say he wanted to help with the country's drug problem. He said back then Elvis wasn't a drinker or a drug user even though everybody thought he probably was. He said all his life until he died Elvis was a nice boy. My boss said Elvis was so nice that he—my boss—probably wouldn't have liked him. But he said he had to give Elvis credit for being a great American. What Elvis did that really convinced my boss how nice he was was that he had teenage girls visit his house all the time but he never had sex with them. He liked to have those girls in his bedroom with their pajamas on, he liked to cuddle with those girls in his bed and talk with them and sometimes sing to them. What Elvis really especially liked, my boss told me, was for those girls to wear white panties. He bought white panties for them. But he wouldn't have sex with them. Even when they wanted to, my boss said, Elvis wouldn't.

"So my job was to be a personal assistant for my boss.

It took him some days to explain to me what my duties were and to teach me how to do them. It was maybe a whole week that he just talked to me about Elvis Presley, so that I would understand that he—my boss—was really nice in the way that he thought Elvis was nice. At first I didn't believe he didn't want sex from me—I was used to how men are, and to me it didn't matter, sex or no sex. But then after some time I did believe him. And my feelings weren't hurt, because my boss was not what you would call attractive. But he liked me, and he was really nice—maybe nice not even in the way he tried to make me think he was nice. He didn't know that he cared about me, but I could feel it. And if I was his personal assistant, then my job was just what he said it was. I never argued.

"Every night I picked out his clothes for the next day and set them out for him to see. I helped him get dressed, I helped him get undressed. I set out fresh pajamas for him at night when he went to bed, I let him read to me after he'd settled himself under the covers, and I talked with him sometimes until it was very late. Then he would ask me to tickle his back so that he could get to sleep. He would turn on his side and ask me to lift his pajama top and run my fingers very lightly over his back. Yes, I know, that was very intimate, but I didn't mind—the tickling was easy, and he was so polite when he asked that of me. His back was big enough that there was a lot of it to tickle.

"Also I loved the reading we did together, especially the book called *100 People Who Are Screwing Up America*. I laughed at that one until he asked me to stop. I liked his voice. I liked when he asked me to read to him and helped me with the words I didn't know. From him I learned *phenomenal, adversity,* and *sweepstakes*. All of the duties were—I don't know how to explain except to say that what I had to do mostly seemed like what you would do for somebody because you really liked that person."

Maura and I simply nodded. Kira was clearly caught up in what she had to say about her boss, and we weren't about to interrupt her.

"I helped him when he took a shower. I scrubbed his back and his foot soles. I washed each of his toes and each of his fingers. While he sat on a stool, I washed his hair and massaged his scalp. And when he got out of the shower I dried him all over. Mostly he and I did not talk in those times—very businesslike and professional is how we were. Even when I helped him stand up or sit down, he was careful about how he touched me.

"He said he wanted to teach me to shave him, but by that time of the morning he was always in too much of a hurry to let me try using the razor on him. He said he didn't want to go to work with his face all bloody—people would ask him what had happened. But he did like me to trim his nails, help him dress, fix his clothes just so, and brush his hair. When it was time for him to leave the house, he stood before me like a soldier. He wanted me to look him over very carefully. The once-over he called it. Then he wanted his good-bye kiss. On the mouth. It was the only time he ever kissed me, and always that kiss was very innocent and very fast. But on the mouth, not on the cheek—that was important to him, he said. That kiss put him in the mood to go to his job at the radio station, he said. Takes all my energy to fire up those sleepy people, he said. Half the people in America wouldn't have a thought in their heads if it weren't for me, he said.

"Every morning I ate breakfast at the table across from

him. The cook waited on both of us in the kitchen—she fixed whatever we asked for, almost always waffles for me and sausage and eggs for him. The cook liked me, and I liked her. I had the impression that he talked with her when I wasn't around. She knew all about my duties, and she liked it that I didn't try to make my boss have sex with me. She said there had been girls before me who had done that. He took the sex, she said, but then he fired them after a week or two. The cook was friendly enough, but she and I kept our distance. She did not try to be my mother—she said she had enough to worry about with her own children."

Kira said that sometimes she ate lunch with her boss, but not very often, and she almost never had dinner with him. She told us that he went out with people or he invited people to his house for parties. He told Kira that he didn't want her to have to see how he acted when he was with the public. She thought it was strange that he invited people who weren't his friends into his home. "The public" is what she said he called those people. Once when she asked him who his friends were, he looked at her and winked and said, "The cook. She's my only friend."

"Once in the shower, when my boss was sitting on the stool and I was scrubbing his back, he asked about my mother—what did I remember about her? He had never asked me anything like that. At first I could not recall my mother—I couldn't see her in my mind because I had not thought of her for so long. And nobody had ever asked me about her before. I started to tell him that I couldn't remember anything about her, but then I did remember a little song I think she sang. I couldn't bring back the words—they must have been Russian words, so I wouldn't have known what they meant anyway. But the tune came back to me a little, and while I stood behind him with my hands on his shoulders I tried to sing it for him. Just, you know, a dum-de-dum kind of singing. Very soft and only for maybe half a minute, because I felt shy about my voice. Nobody would ever think I'm a singer, but for some reason I must have hummed that old song in a way that sounded nice to his ears. When I felt his shoulders shaking, I realized he was crying.

"All of a sudden he stood up, and said come on. He wanted me to follow him, and so I did. He grabbed his towel off its hook and wrapped it around his big waist. I took one, too, and tried to keep from dripping on the floor and the carpets. We walked quickly through his bedroom and down the hall through the big living room, then down another hall toward his office. He told me to wait in the hallway while he went inside. He came back with a key and unlocked a door right beside his office. When we walked in and he switched on the lights, I could see that this was nothing like the other rooms of his house. Here I was in an old-fashioned parlor with high-backed chairs, a loveseat with a coffee table in front of it, little side-tables with picture frames on doilies and knick-knacks. Bookshelves were on either side of a fireplace with a big oil-painted portrait of a handsome woman over it. Old-fashioned picture frames of all sizes were placed all around the room. In a corner was a writing desk, with more framed pictures of his family. In another minute, I understood that this was his special room for pictures of his mother. Everything was very tidy and clean.

"My boss was naked except for his towel wrapped around his waist, I was in the old swimsuit I wore for my boss's showers, I had my towel over my shoulders, and we walked slowly together around the room. When he stopped to look at a photograph, I stopped, too. He would say things like, 'This was when we lived on Merriweather Street,' or 'This was when we visited my grandparents in Arkansas,' or 'This was just before she walked me to my first day of school.' These things he said in a low whisper, and his voice was very beautiful. When we stood in front of the big portrait over the fireplace, he seemed to be talking to the picture more than he was to me. 'My father was always very disappointed in me,' he said, 'but she never was.' He lifted his hand toward the portrait over the fireplace. Then we were both quiet. I felt like we had been in that room a very long time before he led me back out into the hallway, locked the door again and took the key back into his office. It couldn't have been all that long, though, because then we went back to the shower, and finished up our business in there the same as we did every morning."

Kira said every night her boss got down on his knees to say a prayer aloud. She asked him if he wanted her to get down on her knees, too, beside him, and he said no, he didn't want that, but he did want her to stay with him, to sit on the bed right beside where he knelt, and listen to him. She said she didn't mind. "It was the same prayer every night, one that he told me every family in America knew back when he was growing up. I heard it so many times I knew all the words. Before my boss died, I sometimes said the prayer at night when I went to my own room to go to bed. I don't know why, I never got down on my knees the way he did. But since he died, I do it. I get down on the floor, put my elbows on the bed, and clasp my hands in front of my chin. It feels strange, and I don't think God hears me or cares if I say the prayer or don't. But if my boss could hear me, I know it would please him. *Now I lay me down to sleep*, I say, and the words bring him into my mind.

"He did sometimes tell me about how he thought he might die soon. He said he knew he wasn't taking care of himself the way he should. He had lived hard, he said. And he said he wouldn't be surprised if somebody tried to kill him. 'Not everybody out there loves me,' he said. He said he paid his body-guards to keep him from getting shot, but he didn't think they could protect him if somebody really wanted to kill him. 'A shooter in a window can kill anybody,' he said. He told me that if he died or somebody killed him, people like you"—Kira nodded at us to show that she meant Maura and me—"would come here and try to talk to me. 'Media people,' he said. They'll eventually find you and show up, he told me. 'They'll come here from New York,' he said. 'And you know what?' he said. 'I want you to talk to them. I want you to tell them everything you know about your old boss. Tell them about your job and what you did in this house. Tell them every bit of it. Then tell them to write it up just the way you told it to them. Tell them if they don't get it right, you'll come looking for them.'"

⌘

Back in our room at the Brazilian Court, without stopping the little machine and without talking, Maura and I listened to the recording all the way through to the end. We did this during the cocktail hour, though we did not have cocktails. We both felt an urgent need to hear Kira's words again. I mostly watched Maura, who kept her eyes closed. But here and there in the story, she opened her eyes and checked my face, as if to assure herself that I was hearing what she was hearing. At the very end, when Kira stopped speaking and the recorder shut itself off, we sat without saying anything.

In the silence a stray thought sneaked into my mind. Maybe the girl had affected us so strongly because for weeks on end we'd had almost nothing to do with anyone except each other. We'd lived as if we had the world to ourselves.

I finally spoke up. "Hard not to believe he planned it, don't you think? Find a girl who would tell his story to make him look like a super-hero. You think he picked her out just because he knew he could trick her into believing he was a great guy?"

Maura shook her head and grimaced. "I think he made it up as he went along," she said. "He picked her out for sex, but then when he had her in the house, he got another idea about what to do with her."

I didn't want to say so, but I thought Maura was right. "Okay," I said.

After she saw that I wasn't going to argue with her, she went on. "What I wonder," she said, "is what *she* makes of it. She hasn't sorted it out? Or she was sorting it out while she was telling it to us?"

"I believed her the whole time she was talking," I said. "I don't think she held anything back. I think what she makes of it is exactly what she told us. She's shocked, she's sad, she's grieving."

Maura studied me. "She's a very smart girl. Smart in a

way that you and I can't imagine because our childhoods were not battles to survive. My issue is that I can't believe a person who's been through what she has would be so naïve about him."

Now it was my turn to study Maura. "Maybe it's because I'm a man," I said. "It makes perfect sense to me that he was two different people—the monster we murdered, and the man who was kind to Kira and who gave her a life in this country. She accepted him for what he was when the two of them were together. *Because* of what she had gone through, she accepted Hatemo as generous and decent."

"And only mildly perverted," Maura muttered.

"That made him all the more persuasive to her," I said. "If he'd been a saint around her, she'd have distrusted him immediately."

We just sat quietly. Then Maura stood up and walked out onto our room's balcony. We were ten floors up with a view of the beach and the ocean. When I followed her out, she moved over a step to make room beside her at the railing. It was still hot out there even though it was almost sundown. There was a definite breeze up where we were, but it had no cooling power. The ocean, the beach, the coppery light, the strip directly beneath us, in that moment all of it looked as eerie as outer space, and Maura suddenly seemed strange, too, with the warm little wind swirling her hair around her head. Palm Beach made her look like the alien version of herself. It was a mystery to me why anyone would want to live in a place like this.

"You didn't ask her to tell us about how he died," I said.

She was quick to answer. "I kept meaning to ask her, but then after she told her story, I realized I didn't want to hear her describe it. It's what I came down here for, but then I saw it wasn't what I wanted after all."

I nodded, but she didn't notice. I let a little time pass before I said, "Why don't we change our flight to talk to her again? And fly back home tomorrow afternoon?"

"So what did I get?" Maura turned to face me. "Out of this?" She flapped her hand out toward the ocean as if it owed her an explanation. Her face looked a little flushed in this light, and I saw that she was more than a little stirred up. "This vile old creature was two people—that's what you're telling me, and I think you're right. But what am I supposed to do with that?"

I knew the answer immediately, but I made myself think about it for at least half a minute. Correct is not the point here. The point is how to get the two of us back to where we need to be with each other. Realignment is the goal.

"Nothing," I finally said. "Two people. We wiped them both out."

She nodded, her jaw still tight. "Two for one," she said. "Maybe three, if you count the Kira who was a personal assistant. That person went poof when Hatemo stopped breathing."

"Three, yes," I said. I paused a beat or two before I asked, "Feel any better? Or worse?"

"I don't know," she said, looking up into the crazy wind and the gaudy sky. "But can we go back in there and you just hold me for a while? I need to cry, but I'm not sure I can do it by myself."

"I can do that," I told her. I really liked being able to say it with conviction.

⌘

Next morning we decided to be tourists. We didn't say so, but we both felt the need to put Dr. Hatemo and Kira Gregorevna out of our thoughts. We had plenty of time before we had to head to the airport, so we put on our recently purchased swimsuits and our hotel robes, sunglasses, hats, and sandals. We headed to the beach.

We had in mind just to put up our rented umbrella right in front of the hotel and hang out on the sand for an hour or two. I was working on making a comfortable little beach area for us when I found Maura standing perfectly still and staring up the beach as if she was trying to pick somebody out from the crowd scattered around the public area.

"You think she's up that way?" I asked.

"Yes," she said. "I'd bet money on it. How long do you think it would take us to walk that far?"

"Ten minutes," I said. "Maybe fifteen." I probably wanted to see if Kira was sitting on her bench just as much as Maura did.

It was an easy decision. We just fell in beside each other, and started hiking. "We're probably going to get sunburnt," I said.

Maura grunted. "Walk fast," she said. "That way the sun won't get that much of us."

"This is science?" I asked.

"Trust me," she said.

Kira Gregorevna was there. She was definitely there. In no disguise whatsoever. If before today she'd been dressing to keep people from noticing her, this morning she'd gone in the opposite direction. She'd stationed herself on the sand only a few yards from her usual bench. What little there was of her bikini was a bright shade of raspberry that caught your eye. Kira was here all right, long-legged, healthy, tanned, she was so vivid you wondered where the TV cameras were. Her hair shimmered in the sunlight like antique gold, and she looked fourteen or fifteen at most. I was astonished at her ability to change her appearance. The other beach folks were keeping their distance. Eyes shaded, she was propped on her elbows on a navy blue towel, scanning the people who passed by her. When we approached, she lifted her sunglasses and flashed us a welcoming smile. "Hello there," she called.

"Hello, Kira," Maura and I replied almost in unison. I was ready to stop and speak to Kira politely, but Maura didn't slow down. "Keep walking," she murmured.

"Nice to see you," Kira called. Her voice was plaintive. Her lifted hand quickly lost altitude when she saw that we were not stopping to chat.

"Nice to see you, too," we called back to her.

LOVE IN SEPTEMBER

On the flight home Maura and I had hardly any conversation—even during our layover in Atlanta—and yet we
seemed newly affectionate with each other. The affection
itself was of the physical variety—little touches of the
palms or fingertips, some bumping of hips, elbows, and
shoulders. On two occasions while we were killing time
by strolling through the Atlanta airport, Maura, who was
less inclined to such behavior than I was, brushed her
hand down my back. The second time I could have sworn
that she let her hand pass down along my derriere. If she'd
done that weeks ago when we were so ridiculously hot for
each other, I'd have taken it for desire. But in that earlier
time desire embarrassed her too much to allow her to do
such a thing. There in the airport she was just copping
a friendly feel. *Use your words*, I was tempted to tell her
immediately after she did it, but I was savoring the mood
we'd fallen into—a benign silence like lake water calming
after high winds.

In Florida we had stayed out on the beach a little
longer than we should have, but we weren't really burnt.
We'd been under the sun just long enough to awaken
our long napping skin. Strapped into our airplane seats,
our bodies took up the task of communicating silently, a

happy replacement for the words upon which we ordinarily relied.

Taking a taxi from Reagan back to Maura's place in Georgetown that day, I decided that the city looked especially amiable. It was mid-afternoon, the early September sunlight had deepened and softened in the days since our departure, and a cosmic forgiveness seemed to be in the air. College students were out sitting at the sidewalk tables of coffee shops and cafes, while bus stops were animated by day-school kids, teasing and twittering. I imagined Maura must have been taking the same pleasure I was from those street scenes. In the cab's back seat we'd moved a little closer to each other than we'd ordinarily sit. "This is a nice town where we live, don't you think?" I murmured. She turned a friendly face to me and nodded, though it was evident her thoughts were elsewhere. I didn't mind. Some thoughts of my own had arisen. Even before our trip to Florida I'd had a notion about our living arrangements, and this seemed the right time to run it by Maura.

"Do you think I should sell my condo or just sublet it?" I asked her. No sooner had I released the words—and there was no urgency to my tone—than I realized the question might have deeper implications than I had considered. Did I mean to be asking her what she thought of the two of us growing old together or whether we should start looking for a cemetery where we might be buried beside each other? The sudden darkness of those thoughts sent a jolt of panic to my chest, and I sat up straight so as to receive Maura's reply—regardless of what it would be—with all due gravity.

But it was my sociable tone that Maura read, rather than the question of whether she wanted my company to walk through the valley of the shadow of death. When she turned again to face me, her expression had gone dreamy. "Hum," she said. "Maybe so." She kept staring at me, though I doubted she had noticed the spike of panic I'd just experienced. "Do you know what I really want to do, Jack?" she asked.

I shook my head.

"I want to go on a road trip. I want to take a car trip with you. I've got a desire for the open road. I want to see some nature. I want to walk on some dirt paths and spend some time with you someplace where there are lots of trees and not another human being in sight."

I studied her face. I was pretty sure there was no hidden agenda in her words. She wanted just what she said she wanted. And right then the idea of a road trip with Maura appealed to me more than going to look at cemetery plots. "All right," I said, sitting back and relaxing. "Let's do it. One good thing about being out with the deer and the raccoons is that we probably won't be feeling the need to eliminate any right-wing crazies."

"Ha!" she said.

⌘

Maura's hankering for the highway awakened an old remembrance in me. If you thought about it, the idea of a road trip was the opposite of the impulse to kill somebody. To kill took determination and focus, whereas to take a road trip you just needed to embrace vagueness of purpose. Until Maura revealed to me her successful assassination of Bashar al-Assad I'd long considered myself to be a person of no consequence. However, her request that I name her next victim had brought up in me my profound detestation of the Supreme Court Justice, and once I had sounded his name aloud for her to hear, there I was, as much a killer as Cain or Jesse James or John Wilkes Booth.

In my third week in the army some twenty-four years ago, at Fort Jackson, South Carolina, a bayonet instructor had called me out for butt-stroking the training dummy with inadequate conviction. "Son," he told me, stepping up close enough to get in my face, "all you did was just make that asshole mad." He gestured toward the dummy. "You have to stroke the son of a bitch like you want to air mail his skull back home to your mama." Instead of meeting the sergeant's eyes, I studied his nametag, which read, "Dutton." To demonstrate, he took my rifle from my hands, gave me a conspiratorial look, then turned to use my rifle butt to strike the enemy dummy with such force it sounded like a truck colliding with a tree.

"Try it again, son," he said, handing me back my rifle. My second butt-stroke was notably harder than my first, but compared to the instructor's mighty blow it was little more than a feeble swatting of the dummy's left jaw. Sergeant Dutton laughed out loud at me as he marked something on his clipboard. "Son, I'm going to fail you for the butt-stroke part of this training course," he said. "And I'll be doing you a favor, because you don't want to be anywhere near a combat situation. You want to be sitting somewhere behind a desk. I just took care of you right here," he said and tapped his clipboard with his pen. "You gonna live to a ripe old age, son. All because of me and this here clipboard."

While we made our plans to go on the road I considered telling Maura about my encounter with the bayonet instructor. But the moral of the story was that Sergeant Dutton showed me that I did not have it in me to be a killer, whereas she, Maura Nelson, the nerdy lady from Clarksville, Tennessee, had made a notable correction in my self-perception: I did in fact have what it took to kill another human being. Or at least it seemed that way. Didn't I have two notches on my conscience, one for Justice Nino and another for Dr. Hatemo? But the tantalizing conclusion—and it was one that neither Maura nor I wanted to reach—was that without her I was no killer at all. I was merely her accessory. Though I knew she wished me to be equally responsible, so far the impetus to kill had been all hers. I had participated only as a sounding board to help her gain purpose and focus. I had supplied a name, or I had nodded in agreement. Maura had committed the act.

So I didn't have the nerve to take up the discussion with her. And I wasn't sure I had the nerve to work through the ethics of that even in the privacy of my own thoughts. Either I was a full-fledged killer and therefore entitled to be Maura's companion, or I was merely a follower and therefore destined to lose my place in Maura's life. Which was what I most valued in my own life.

The situation rip-sawed me. Our mood—or our shared aura—had become so sweet and our road-trip plan was so liberating that I knew I'd be a fool to start up a conversation that could only lead to gloom and diminishment. I half expected Maura to pick up the unintentional signals my interior life must have been emitting. But either there were no such signals or Maura was too cheerily preoccupied to be able to receive them.

⌘

"I heard myself informing the Enterprise agent on the phone that I wanted a car with a killer stereo," Maura told me. The rental she had chosen was a Mercedes with a sound system that would rival Carnegie Hall's. Turned out that before she made the discovery that had changed both our lives, she had been sort of haphazardly building a vast iTunes music library. The discovery—and her application of it to Bashar Al-Assad—had distracted her from music altogether. Only when the Enterprise agent answered the phone did she remember the thousands of songs she'd collected over the years. Then it came to her that we could listen to her music while we took our tour. "I think I want the music as much as I do the traveling," she said. "I always wanted somebody to listen with me to the songs I loved. I'd get all teary-eyed over 'Thunder Road,' and it would be like I hadn't really completely felt what I thought I had felt because there wasn't anybody with me to talk about it. Or even just to look at to see if that person was feeling what I was."

Our goal was to drive the Blue Ridge Parkway until we felt like turning back. From Georgetown we set out for Winchester, Virginia, where Maura said she wanted to set her feet on the floor of Patsy Cline's childhood home. "I only like about four of her songs," Maura explained to me, "but I really like those four." We'd made it beyond the beltway, heading west on Route 50, and Maura had taken the first shift of driving. "Do you know 'I Fall to Pieces'?" she asked me. Then she snorted and said, "I'm sure you know it, everybody does. But what I mean is, do you just about fall to pieces when you hear those first words of the song?" And she sang the words for me.

This was a first, Maura singing to me. Her voice was nothing special—adequate to the task is how I would describe it. She grinned when she stopped, as if she intended her singing to be a kind of a joke. Which it was. But the aching timbre of her voice managed to make me hear what she was talking about—longtime deep heartbreak sounded in four simple words, four easy notes probably in the key of C. If I had been by myself listening to Patsy Cline—even on the Mercedes's sound system—I doubt that I'd have turned the volume up or noticed what the song was or who was singing it. In the company of my new companion of the road, just from her singing those four quavering notes, I suddenly understood what I might be in for on our trip. It occurred to me that maybe I had never had the experience of "feeling" a song with somebody else.

⌘

Winchester, Virginia, is a town where you need to have a destination or else there's not much point to being there. It's got this very sleepy aura that suggests progress stopped happening here around 1955 and everybody decided to take a nap. Every house and lawn looks like it's owned by a Republican retiree with a yard boy to tend to it. "Lord, don't let us get stuck here," I murmured when we turned onto Kent Street, where the great singer survived her childhood. Maura murmured, "Amen."

In Patsy's creaky old house, Maura stayed close by my

side, even holding onto my arm here and there, so that I almost felt like I was living some of Patsy's life through Maura's imagining of the ten-year-old girl sitting at that kitchen table to do her homework and then climbing those steps up to her bedroom. Maura kept her voice low even though we had the house pretty much to ourselves. "You know she discovered she had that big voice after she got rheumatic fever and had to go to the hospital," she told me. A little later we ordered grilled cheese sandwiches and tomato soup for lunch at the Triangle Diner, where Patsy worked as a waitress while she was in high school. We put quarters in the table-top jukebox selector and listened to "Walkin' After Midnight," "Crazy," and "She's Got You." By the time we left the place, every customer had found somewhere else to go, and all the waitresses except ours had gone out back for a smoke.

Truth is, out in the parking lot I realized I had maxxed out on Patsy Cline in the Triangle Diner. I felt the need to tell Maura about it, and I did so in the car as we departed Winchester on the way down to Front Royal, where we would be spending the night. It was my turn to drive, and maybe it was the Mercedes that empowered me to speak my mind. It's one thing to sit in the passenger seat and keep your opinions to yourself, but driving a Mercedes you could never afford to buy will make you feel like you're a person who ought to share his thoughts with the world. I told Maura that Patsy was new for me, and so even though I had had enough of her, I nevertheless appreciated the way she—Maura—had given me a sense of the whole life of a person I'd known nothing about before that morning. "But Patsy doesn't break my heart the way she does yours," I told her. Something had gotten into me that I didn't quite understand, but I was proud of myself for speaking aloud an abrasive truth. I was also pleased to think I probably wouldn't have any more Patsy Cline coming at me for the rest of the day. Plus it suited me just fine to be putting Winchester in the rear-view mirror. Just the right perspective for this town was the thought that came to me.

"I'm okay with that, Jack," Maura said, surprising me with how pleasant her voice was. "It's more like Patsy breaks my heart by getting killed when she was thirty-one years old in an airplane crash. And I add that fact into what I hear when I listen to a song of hers. There are maybe a dozen singers I'd put ahead of her as heartbreakers. But Patsy is essential to me—and to most people who listen hard to music." She turned her face to me. "You get that, don't you?"

I told her that I did, and I wasn't lying. I thanked her for the crash-course. We were leaving Winchester and getting to some open countryside on Route 522. There were cattle to be seen alongside the highway, but they had the appearance of having been groomed before they were sent out to graze. Maura was staring out her window but then, as if an idea had suddenly come to her, she started fiddling with her iPod. In a moment she punched the device with her forefinger and announced, "*This* is a song that breaks my heart. And I don't know a darn thing about the people who sing it." Maura's "darn" amused me enough that I intended to tell her so, but then the song began, and I knew I should listen or risk hurting Maura's feelings.

I heard a man and a woman singing a kind of harmony I wasn't used to hearing, bluegrass I guessed, but a slow ballad that seemed to be about some kids who were waiting for their parents to find them. *I have their letter in my pocket…/ the darkness and cold drawing near.* I was trying to pick up the story line, but it was the sound of those voices that took hold of my thoughts. The woman was the lead singer, but the man's voice was a high tenor that shadowed her contralto so closely that the two of them sounded to my ear unnaturally intertwined.…*they look for my face in the crowd.* Their harmony generated a feeling of sadness that affected a region somewhere in the vicinity of my throat.

I became intensely aware of Maura beside me, and I deliberately kept my eyes on the road because I was pretty sure she was even more caught up in that song than I was. *We gave them our four pounds and twenty.* To tell the truth I felt like I was on the edge of a great canyon of emotion into which I would plummet unless I switched off the music. *They look for my face in the crowd / It's been so long since they've seen me.* Okay, I couldn't help it, a sob insisted on making it up out of my belly and chest, even though I did my best to stifle it. *And I wonder if they'll know me now.*

I didn't like what was happening to me, but I knew I had to look at Maura. I did it. She was looking back at me, and she had tears streaming down both her cheeks. So I didn't feel so bad about crying, even though—maybe because Maura was crying silently—I really didn't want to make any sobbing sounds.

"Do you want to pull over for a minute?" she murmured.

I needed to hold in the crying when I answered. "I do, but I don't," I rasped out. And kept driving.

"Conundrum," she said when the song came to an end.

"Yes," I said. I took a deep breath and knew that I was all right. But I also wondered how many more songs Maura had on that iPod that were going to rattle me around like that one. Getting weepy was not what I wanted when I listened to music.

⌘

"Really sappy song," I told Maura just as we were crossing the bridge over the Shenandoah River. Whatever had gotten into me, I felt like a correction of some kind needed to be made. Since we were coming into Front Royal, I knew we wouldn't be in the car much longer. "I don't know if I can stand to listen to it again."

Her expression seemed to inform me that I was as pitiful and weak as I felt right then. It was the first time she'd ever given me a look like that, and it riled me up even more than I already was.

"I'm not somebody who cries in the car," I said. My voice was much more insistent that I meant it to be.

"Where exactly do you do your crying, Jack?" she asked softly.

"I don't," I snapped at her. It occurred to me that I had never before felt anything even close to anger at her, but I felt like I was the one who was in the right. I wasn't about to back down.

"I thought so," she said and turned her face toward her window.

Front Royal must be Winchester's first cousin from the black sheep side of the family—it's a town that whispers, *Forget me*, in every direction you look. We stayed quiet until the GPS that came with the Mercedes directed us into the parking lot of the Killahevlin B&B. And even when we were carrying our luggage and computer cases into the place, we tried to manage with as few words as possible. The lobby was lovely—old and elegantly quaint—and the host, Tom Conkey, was chatty, which was just what we needed because we could exchange small talk with Tom without having to speak to each other.

In the room, too, we puttered around in silence a good five minutes without speaking. I finally sat down at the desk to connect my tablet with the Killahevlin's WiFi system. I hadn't been there long before I sensed that Maura was standing just behind me. The room was very quiet. I turned to face her.

"I have something to tell you," she said. "I've thought about this, and I know it's a little crazy, but I'm pretty sure it's right. At least it's right for me." She wasn't mad, but her grave voice meant to let me know she was serious. "I've killed three people," she said. "You've helped me kill two of them. We're murderers. We're criminals. First degree murderers, because we thought about it before we did it. With Nino we might have set the record for premeditation. We may very well go to prison. Maybe even the electric chair, or whatever it is they use nowadays to execute people like us. But even though neither you nor I think we're in the wrong, we don't have a leg to stand on."

I closed up my tablet and turned directly to her. "I don't know where this is going, Maura," I said.

Something in her face told me she had this little moment of pitying me. "Right here," she said. "A song in the car just moved us to tears. Both of us. We two killers just wept because a piece of music about lost children needing their parents made us feel for them very deeply."

I took a moment to try to guess what her point was going to be. "I don't think that means anything, Maura," I told her. "Or whatever it means can't be of any use or comfort to us. The Nazis who put hundreds of Jews to death every day went back to their rooms after work and listened to Bach and Mozart. They wept, too."

"I know that," she said. "I've been struggling with that. Here's the difference. They wanted to kill an entire race of people—men, women, children, babies. They killed because of a concept they'd embraced. What was monstrous about it was that they could think of it as nothing personal."

"And we? Out of what do we kill? I'm not arguing or even debating with you, Maura. I really do want you to tell me what the God-damn hell we're doing."

"Individuals. Specific persons."

"And why is that special?"

"Well, we don't get to do it legally. We'll go to prison if they catch us. But just as a judge or a jury makes a decision, we've decided these people do great harm. They will keep on doing it unless we stop them. We decide that a specific person needs to die. For us it's personal."

"Okay," I said. "I'll have to think about what that means. But right now, if anything, it makes me feel worse."

"My point exactly," she said. "We need to feel worse. We need to feel these deaths the way we felt that song. Except a hundred times more intensely. We need to carry each one of these deaths on our backs. Everywhere we go."

I just stared at her.

She didn't look away. "Yes," she said.

"So this is what will make it all right?" I said. My voice wasn't steady, but I went on anyway. "If we make ourselves feel these deaths completely? If we carry them around with us?"

She stared hard at me for nearly a full minute. "It can't ever be all right. To you or me or anybody."

"So maybe this will stop us?" I asked her.

"I don't think so," she said.

"Now I'm the one who hates us," I told her.

We stared at each other.

Finally Maura shrugged and turned away.

⌘

Maura and I behaved like chastened children. We tried to cheer ourselves up with one of the bottles of wine we'd brought from DC to have with us in our hotel rooms. We sipped in silence. Then we drove to dinner at Vino e Formaggio. There we had more wine and then food, and though we tried, we couldn't exchange more than a few words. Then a thought came to me that I blurted aloud before I had time to think it through. "What about if we split?"

"Good question." Maura's tone made me understand she had already been mulling it over. "We can't know for sure, but I'd say that if we split, you'll definitely stop. Unless you figure out the method on your own how it's done. And I think figuring out the exact method is the last thing you want to do."

I took a moment to process that. She wasn't wrong. So I nodded. "What about you?"

"I'd stop," she said. She held my eyes with hers. "I need you. You know that. I need you to be in it with me."

I was shocked at how my heart fluttered like flag in

the breeze in response to the words *I need you.* Even so, I tried not to show how much I was affected by what she'd said. I pushed the discussion forward. "So that's how we could put a stop to us?" I said. "Split?"

"Yes," she said, and she didn't look away.

"You might find somebody else. A replacement."

Maura shook her head. Didn't look away.

I studied her face. I believed her.

Neither of us had eaten more than a bite or two. Our waiter took our plates away and asked if we wanted dessert.

"Yes," I told him. "One tiramisu. Two forks," I said. "The lady and I will split it."

Maura smiled. When the waiter brought the tiramisu, we set upon it.

⌘

Like high school or college kids, we were in a hurry to slip back into our room in the Killahevlin. Once we were inside we left the lights off and couldn't get undressed fast enough. Evidently our sex life had been waiting for us to rediscover our best selves. We'd been taking our time, maybe being a little too patient with each other, settling for pretty good or okay lovemaking. That evening we were right back where we were when Maura declared us to be really good fuckers. Sweaty and panting we finally broke away from each other and splayed our naked selves out on either side of the king-size bed. "Marvin Gaye knew what he was singing about," I said, and Maura actually giggled. Probably more to communicate solidarity with me than because of my sense of humor, but I appreciated the response. I translated her giggle to mean exactly what I had been thinking: *This closeness with you right here in this room and on this bed is why you and I are never going to split.* I had needed to hear Maura say she needed me, and now that she had said it, I didn't think I needed anything else.

I turned toward her to snuggle, and she was in the mood for it. But she plucked the remote off the table on her side of the bed and clicked the TV on even as we were nestling up with each other. "Rachel," she said. "I want her to see us on this bed. I want her blessing," she said, and I snorted. We both had a thing for Rachel Maddow, though we did agree that she could be repetitive when the day's politics hadn't given her much to work with. Maura clicked through the channels until she found MSNBC, then she leaned away from me to set the remote back on the table.

It wasn't quite time for Rachel, and neither of us much cared for Ed Schultz, but we left him on with the sound turned low. Our post-coital snuggling had most of our attention. But then we heard a voice that was familiar to us, so when Maura lifted her head to see who was speaking, I did, too. "I forgot she was testifying today," Maura said.

We fixed our pillows to prop us up to see what the Secretary of State had to say to the congressional committee. She was wearing glasses, and we knew she was still recovering from the concussion she had suffered a couple of weeks ago, but she looked healthy, and her voice was strong. "God, I love that woman," Maura said. "I didn't used to, but I do now."

When the camera switched to a young senator who also looked familiar to us, a curly haired fellow about my age, it took us a minute or so to remember who he was.

When Maura pointed the remote and turned the sound up, I felt her body go tense. The Senator from Kentucky was saying, "...the culpability for the worst tragedy since 9/11...and I really mean that. Had I been president at the time, and I found that you did not read the cables...."

Maura and I pulled farther away from each other and sat up straight just in time to hear the Senator tell the Secretary of State, "I would have relieved you of your position...."

"Switch it off," I murmured. "This guy's an idiot." As if she needed to take a particular stance in order to shut down the Senator, Maura stood up beside the bed with the remote in her hand pointing at the TV. But she didn't push the button. She just stood there, pointing the thing, as if this senator had turned her into a statue. And maybe I wouldn't have turned him off either. Repulsive as it was to listen to that jackass, I wanted to see how Madame Secretary handled this. More particularly I wanted to see and hear Harriet Lee respond to him. I wanted to see her incinerate him in front of the whole nation. Her face, however, with its forced smile and her slightly nodding head, informed me that she was going to suffer this fool all the way to the end of his lecture. "...really cost these people their lives...had someone been more on top of the job—and I don't mean to suggest...," he went on. "...I don't suspect your motives of wanting to serve your country...."

I rousted myself from the bed, walked around it, stood close beside Maura, and put my arm around her. Then I gently removed the remote from her hand. She let it go easily and dropped her hand to her side. She leaned into me, and we stood beside each to listen to the Senator drone on. Finally he asked the Secretary of State a question about "transferring weapons to Turkey out of Libya."

The silence that followed the Senator's question was a moment of high political intensity. The camera switched to the face of the Secretary of State. She looked out through the TV set to Maura and me standing in the dark waiting for her to humiliate that Tea Party moron in front of TV watchers all across the nation. Instead of outrage and fury, however, she was bemused. She asked, "To Turkey?" in such a way as to indicate that she knew he had posed a wacko question to her, but her voice was immensely precise. Her tone made clear that all the drivel he had directed toward her for the past ten minutes had not harmed a hair on her head and that she considered him about as important as the dust under her shoes. But that same tone maintained perfect respect for the Senator. That was a way a politician could express extreme contempt for another politician within the boundaries of decorum. Such poise under the glaring lights of a congressional hearing took years of training. The Secretary of State told the Junior Senator from Kentucky, "I'll have to look into that," in a voice that any astute listener would translate to mean something like, *Sir, though I consider you lower than whale excrement, I nevertheless honor you with the manners required by this occasion.*

Maura turned, walked into the bathroom, and closed the door.

I switched off the TV and stood in the dark. The Secretary of State had demonstrated quintessential savvy and competence—and I deeply appreciated her. She had just shown the entire world what it took for a democracy to function. You don't display anger at your enemy, you don't even get chippy. You just listen to the person whose thinking is repulsive without rolling your eyes or grimacing, and you go on doing your job. Your will and your ability to maintain etiquette are part of what keeps the country's nose above water.

In that moment in the dark I loved that smart and powerful woman. She was the best, and God knew the country needed her. But I suddenly knew the country needed Maura and me, too. After 9/11 and the toxic politics of those past few years—the politics that had empowered the ignorant jerks like that Junior Senator from Kentucky. Madame Secretary was not enough.

DANCE WITH ME UNTIL THE END OF TIME

The next morning when I expected our breakfast conversation to be about the congressional hearings we had seen on TV, Maura began telling me about her brother. She talked with the kind of purposefulness that suggested that sometime between when we had gone to sleep last night and our making our way down to the B&B dining room she had made a decision. Evidently—after all those weeks, during which I had not asked her about her brother out of concern that I'd be bringing up a subject that would trouble her—*this* morning I needed to know about Ben, a.k.a., Doctor Nelson.

"On his sixteenth birthday he was six feet four inches tall," she told me. "That was when I was twelve and a half and barely five feet tall," she said. "So tall and short were pretty much the defining facts of our relationship."

"Maura, is this what you want to talk about right now?" I asked. "I mean, I do of course really want to know anything you want to tell me about your brother, but…"

She shook her head and did her best to grin at me. "So listen," she said. "Ben was a great dancer, and something that made both of us really happy was doing the jitterbug—what they call 'the shag' now, but to us it was never anything but jitterbugging. That high-speed, fancy-footwork kind of goofy body collaboration. He liked nothing better than swinging me around, flipping me over, even tossing me up in the air and then catching me like a rag doll. And I liked nothing better than giving myself over to him and letting him launch me out into the air and make me dizzy.

"My parents got us started because they thought Ben needed exercise and he needed a break from the hours of studying he put in. At school his teachers thought he was a genius, and he might have been, but what he really had a talent for was sitting in a chair and reading and memorizing and making charts and looking things up. He was the kind of genius who works his butt off. So my parents, who'd grown up in the fifties, got out their old Coasters and Bill Haley and Little Richard records and started showing Ben and me how to do the dances they'd learned when they were our age. They weren't surprised that it caught on with me—I'd already taken some ballet, and what eleven- or twelve-year-old girl wouldn't be thrilled to be dancing with her older brother?—but they were shocked that Ben took to it the way he did. They didn't even expect him to have the coordination for it, because he'd had these growth spurts that had made him into Super Klutz when he first went to high school. Turns out Ben must have gotten his coordination while he was memorizing chemical formulas and doing extra reading for his calculus course. His footwork was better than mine, even though I was light on my feet."

"Maura, I…"

She raised her hand. She was not about to let me interrupt her.

"So when Ben and I took up dancing with a passion, my parents kind of kicked back and congratulated themselves. They figured they'd done something smart for their kids, and so they let us alone a lot more than they had been doing. Not only were we getting healthy exercise and learning about American music—Ben had looked up the old swing tunes and bands from the thirties and forties, so we were dancing to Benny Goodman, Count Basie, and Woody Herman and the Thundering Herd—but the two of us had turned into best friends and constant companions. Even now I can remember dinner times when my mother and father were just beaming at the two of us jabbering away about Charles Darwin and Marie Sklodowska-Curie and Rachel Carson. In the course of dancing with each other as much as we did after school, Ben had discovered that I 'knew nothing worth knowing,' as he put it, and so he took it upon himself to help with my education.

"We went from being the classic aliens-to-each-other big brother and little sister to being extremely close. I wish Ben were still alive, because I'd really like to know what it felt like to him to be so intimate with his little sister. I guess he wasn't really a child in any but the legal sense, but I was still so much a kid that the only way he could relate to me—which he did completely!—was to revert back to his kid self. But he also kind of yanked me up out of little girlhood into something like nerdy early adulthood. He didn't tell me to do it, but because they weren't interesting to me any more I put away my roller skates and my 3-D Home Kit and my EZ Steppers. All he had to do was show me this physics problem that was probably way too simple to interest him—'How Many

Balloons Does It Take to Lift a Little Girl?'—and a whole world opened up to me. He also showed me 'Bullet from a Car' and 'Dutch Drawbridge' and a lot of problems like that. And of course because Ben was so gaga over Darwin I got fascinated with him, too."

Maura stopped speaking a moment and chuckled sort of awkwardly. "I see now that Darwin was kind of our go-between," she said. I could actually see her eyes begin looking through me as she moved deeper into her thoughts. I waited her out.

Finally she cast her eyes down toward her half-eaten breakfast. "What I have to tell you here, Jack, is that in Ben I came to know a deeply decent human being. That's what I had in mind to tell you this morning. I thought of it last night while we were watching that stupid Senator harass the Secretary of State. I had to ask myself why I experienced such a fury rising up in me while I listened to him and watched him. Surely that's wrong, I knew that—even though yesterday afternoon I was telling you that our motivation is not a concept, it's a recognition of specifically wrongful human beings. And I know you agree with me that the Senator is as wrongful a person as we're likely to see any time soon. But what I felt toward him was nothing more than sheer meanness. The kind of malice that makes you want to run somebody off the road because they're speeding and weaving in and out of traffic. I had to ask myself how I could think it's acceptable to act on the basis of such a feeling."

"Yes?"

Maura was quiet, and I could see it was because she was troubled by where her story had taken her. "The only reason I can know about Ben's goodness is that I got…"

She took a breath. "I might as well go ahead and use this word," she says. "I became *incestuously* close to him."

When she registered the look I gave her, it broke the spell she was in, and she actually chuckled. "I don't mean that I had sex with my brother," she said in a near whisper. "But I do mean that he and I got crazy close. We'd be talking in his room about Stephen Hawking and he'd start undressing and ask me to come into the bathroom with him so we could keep up the conversation while he took a shower. In the middle of the night, I'd wake up with him climbing into the bed with me to tell me about Euler's formula, and I wouldn't think anything of it because I'd be too caught up in the wild stuff about math that he was whispering to me. Or when our parents took us to the beach the two of us would slip out of the rental house around one or two in the morning to go swimming because he'd heard that people had seen bioluminescence just off the Outer Banks—and of course when we got out onto the beach we just took off our pajamas and went skinny-dipping. So I was, shall we say, acquainted with Ben's body as well as his mind and every aspect of his personality. I didn't have to have sex with my brother, because I was so intimate with him that I was in danger of just disappearing inside him."

"You don't sound remorseful." I, too, kept my voice low, but I grinned at her.

"I'm not!" she said, her voice a little too loud for the breakfast chamber of the Killahevlin. "But maybe I ought to be! God, this stuff has me all riled up!" She looked around, a little wildly, at our fellow diners, who were eating their breakfasts in a normal fashion and who didn't seem to have any interest in us. Then she went on in what I have to describe as a really intense murmur. "I don't know if Ben could have held onto his pure sweetness if he'd had to grow up—and especially if he'd had to grow up and live through Shrub's presidency. All I know is he was so deeply good in his devotion to those scientists he taught me to love and in his passion for that music we danced to. Maybe that's a kind of goodness that can only exist in a teenage boy for about two years maximum. After he's not a kid anymore but before he's forced to become a young man. I tell you, I saw it!" she said. "I lived it!" she said, and this time her voice had risen to the point where several of the other diners turned toward us with semi-polite expressions on their faces.

Maura blushed so deeply that any embarrassment I might have felt was obliterated by the extent to which affection and desire for her rose in me in that moment.

⌘

I was the driver for the first shift that morning, and we were quiet as we left Front Royal and headed up the mountain toward the Skyline Drive. It felt like we'd gone through some kind of challenging experience together. After a while Maura fiddled with her iPod and put on "The Sound of Silence." She said nothing, but her legs, arms, head, even her torso, all registered certain phrases and notes of the song. She was very restrained about those movements, but I knew she was aware of how I could see how much that song affected her. When it was finished, she switched off the stereo and turned to me with a serious face. "I'll go to my grave loving that song," she said. "And the talent of the guy who wrote it."

I nodded and waited for her to say more—I was almost certain she played that particular tune to give us a reason to talk about the hearing we had seen on TV. But apparently I was the one who had to start the conversation, because she had nothing more to say. Instead she paid an unusual amount of attention to the scenery.

"So we're finally going to talk about the Senator and the Secretary of State?" I asked her. She could probably hear in my voice that I wasn't being ironic. I was, however, not about to tell her how that whole exchange on TV felt life changing to me last night and still did that morning.

"No, Jack," she said, "I can't do that right now. I'm sorry to say I've reached the point where I'm scared. Of us. Of how the two of us together make this dynamic where somebody dies if something sets us heading down that track. I think that's what I learned from Kira." Instead of looking at me when she said that, she turned toward her window.

"Say a little more please," I asked her.

She kept staring out her window—and I didn't blame her because the September sunlight made everything look new, like you'd never quite seen it before. "Hatemo was awful. So awful I don't have any regret about putting him down. But I can't help wondering if maybe Kira didn't need him."

"You think the way he was using Kira was okay?"

"No," she said, and then she did turn to me. "I don't think that. But I do think where she is without him is likely to turn into something much worse. No matter what she's been through, she's still a kid. She doesn't have her feet under her, and there's nobody around who can help her with that."

"The lady lawyer. Her attorney," I said. "That very capable woman will help her."

"Yes, maybe," Maura said. Then she put her hand on my knee and leaned as close as the Mercedes console would allow her. "Jack," she said. "That Senator has kids. Three boys," she said. "It's not that I don't want him gone. Maybe even as much as I think you do. It's that I need to find a way for us not to be trapped into doing him in. I'm not trying to fix us permanently. I'm just trying to avoid this one act. I need to feel like we have a choice."

"If we see him again on TV. Or read about something he's done or said…"

"That's right," she said. "Then we might have to do it. Or we might not be able to stop ourselves. But right now we're riding in this elegant car on this sumptuous day, and we can go anywhere and do anything we want. You know that Hemingway story where the guy is trying to talk the girl into having an abortion? Remember, she walks away from him and looks out at the river and the mountains and the fields, and she comes back and tells him, 'We can have all this'…? That's how it is with us, Jack. Look out there. All of this is ours. Right now. Every bit of it."

⌘

I had set the cruise control for fifty, so that in the stealthy Mercedes it felt almost like traveling through space, except that instead of stars and inky blackness, the mountain-top trees and scenic lookouts of Virginia moved toward us then swept past in a slow blur. Maura used the car's great sound system like she was a silent DJ, picking the tunes from her iPod one after the other. We heard Rickie Lee

Jones's "Danny's All-Star Joint," the Talking Heads' "Life During Wartime," Melody Gardot's "Worrisome Heart," and Dave Brubeck's "Blue Rondo a la Turk." Then Maura said she wanted a little break; the music was freaking her out it was so intense. "In this car I feel like the music's coming through my skin. It wears me out," she said. So she switched over to the satellite radio and found NPR.

At first I was only half paying attention. *kindergartner, snatched...school bus by a gunman and...underground bunker....* I was aware that there had been some kind of kidnapping in Alabama. I didn't necessarily want to hear about it, but Maura was leaning forward, so I knew she was paying attention....*gunman boarded a stopped school bus Tuesday...shot the bus driver...Jimmy Lee Dykes....*

"Oh Lord," Maura said. It was the first time I'd heard her use a phrase like that. It must have been her Clarksville childhood coming out....*doesn't trust the government... a Vietnam vet...PTSD...didn't socialize...no contact with anybody.*

"He's got a kid in a bunker," she said. "A five-year-old kid. He's holding him hostage because he wants to make speeches about the government." *...communicating through a drainpipe...stand-off in its third day now...no change....*

Maura's face in that light was just wild with everything swirling around in her—rage, helplessness, fear, nausea— like she was channeling what people all over the country were feeling about the guy. That God-damned American crazy! Her face looked like it was about to burst.

Then her expression changed—and I'd seen that look before. She didn't even have to ask the question. I was locked into her frequency, and I was already slowing down and looking for a place to turn around. She was using her phone to find out how much time it would take us to get back to her place and what was the quickest way to get there.

"Three hours," she said. "Don't speed, please."

"Okay," I said. My voice probably conveyed to her how exhilarated I felt. I was so excited, it was going to be very difficult for me not to push the Mercedes to the max. If I had let the car have its way, it could have probably gotten us to Georgetown in two hours. But there was another dimension to my feelings, and it didn't have anything to do with speed. *Connection*, I guess I'd have called it, because *love* just didn't fit. It was like the difference between *making love* and *fucking*—and in that car with Maura and me on our way to carry out the harsh mission that we both fiercely wanted to accomplish, the feeling was definitely more like *fucking* than *making love*. But then my quickened pulse informed me that what we were up to also felt kind of crazy. The idea came to me that the deranged Vietnam vet holding the kid hostage in a bunker was not the only American Crazy acting out right then.

For a very brief moment that thought sparked some serious disturbance in me. But the next moment bumped me up against the obvious conclusion—Maura and I were what the situation called for. If we were as crazy as the guy in the bunker, then so be it. I was fine with whatever name applied to us, we were the only two people on the face of the planet who could fix the situation. Right then, I'd have called us necessary.

⌘

It also went without saying aloud that I would accompany Maura into the killing room. I realized that that's what I'd been calling it in the privacy of my thoughts. Mostly the door stayed closed, but I had passed when Maura had been in there and left it open. And I had passed by when she wasn't in there and the door was open. But on those occasions, I'd felt this taboo against even standing in the doorway and taking a careful look around. That afternoon when she stepped to the side to let me enter before her, I didn't hesitate. Nor was there any visible reason to be wary of the room—a normal professional person's study. Probably because I was looking for clues, I did note that she had two desktop machines, both of them Mac Pro Twelves, available all over the country for about four thousand bucks each, and there were four supplementary units lined up under her desk.

"Applications," she said, pulling up a second desk chair from the table behind us so that the two us could sit side by side. "Applications are, as you know, available for just about everything, but I had to come up with a couple of my own design. I'm not sure why, but I have a gift for making them." She turned on her desktop, then she reached under the desk for a switch that I assumed activated the supplementary units. "There are three steps to this, Jack, and you'll see that they're completely basic—identifying, locating, and executing." She winced when she named the third step. "I'm sorry, I couldn't think of anything else to call it." When I nodded, she went on. "I'm not going to try to do the slow version for you right now, but you'll probably figure out most of it from watching me." When she started typing in queries, commands, and data, I was almost immediately in the dark about what she was doing, a bafflement she must have discerned from my body language—we were sitting almost elbow to elbow.

She focused on her monitor while she tried to clue me in. "In this case location is not a huge problem, because we know the name of the area where our guy is—Midland City, Alabama. It's always identity that's the most challenging, because I have to come up with the exact DNA. No room for error there. Again this case is easier because our guy was in the service—and I have security access to all those records. So I can find out enough information to get a general fix on him. The conventional wisdom is that DNA is tough to get on somebody unless they agree to let you swab their mouths or give over a hair or a blood sample. But in fact you generate DNA just by breathing and pooping and peeing and even—forgive me for being crude—farting. It's just that…"

Maura typed, paused, snorted to herself, typed again, typed and paused again several times. "There," she said finally. "That's him. Picking up that data is the crucial step nobody's yet seemed to figure out, yet it did come to me—and yes, it's extremely obvious, but evidently that's why nobody's yet stumbled on it the way I did. And the app for it wasn't the easiest I've ever created. But it's in here now"—she patted the Mac Pro Twelve—"and so far, if I give it good information, it has had no trouble finding the target person and validating that person's ID beyond any possibility of doubt." She gave me a look that struck me as both bemused and deeply serious. "No collateral damage," she said softly. "I couldn't stand even the faintest possibility of that."

I didn't have to nod—I saw her reading my face. Our brains had merged so completely that what she said aloud was exactly what I thought as the words came from her mouth.

Maura was quiet then, clearly waiting for the machine to do its work. The map on her monitor focused, re-set, and focused again. The graphics were so sharp and detailed that they appeared to be the work of an artist, and they bore an eerie resemblance to a brain scan. There was a pause when the map reached its final state, then her machine made a little pinging sound, and an orange X lit up on the grid. "And there he is," she said. She tapped the X on the monitor with her fingernail.

She leaned back in her chair and looked at me. "Are you okay?" she asked.

"I hadn't thought about it," I told her. We were both surprised by what I'd said. But it was the plain truth—I'd been so caught up in being there with Maura and watching her and listening to her that I had completely lost track of myself. While she and her technology had identified and located that guy, I had completely lost myself and all sense of where I was. I made a soft humming noise that Maura noted with a quick grimace, then she turned back to her keyboard and her monitor. "We're almost there," she said.

She typed, paused, typed some more, paused, and tapped the keys rapidly. "This is just a laser bouncing off a satellite," she said. "You do need a certain level of clearance to have access to the data, but I've never been able to understand why those guys at the CIA and the KGB haven't figured this out and started using it. All over the world I guess the scientists who study lasers must have decided they'd gone as far as they could go. I had to work out a few more steps on my own. And they weren't that difficult." She shook her head in a silent and private reprimand to the complacent laser scientists.

That was when I decided that Maura's assertion that anybody could figure out how to do this procedure was just a form of modesty on her part. She was not putting on an act—she really did believe that because the discovery came to her, it could come to anybody. But I knew she was wrong. Years later a team of scientists and military technologists would very likely come up with the secret. Until then she was the only living person who knew how to accomplish what we were doing in that room.

"Anyway, we're all set," she said, sliding the mouse over to my side of her desk, then sitting back and turning to me. Her face was absolutely neutral. For all her expression told me she might have just said, "Coffee's ready."

"What do you mean?" I murmured.

She nodded toward the mouse. "Single click," she said.

THE FLATS

When Maura and I walked out of her study I felt like the world had become more hostile to me than it had been before. But I also felt weirdly protected against any real harm. By what I didn't know. Evidently I had stepped into a dimension of my life that had always been there but with which I'd had no previous acquaintance. I tried to understand it while Maura and I walked across her living room and into her kitchen. But my general mood—as far as I could discern it—was a mutated variety of cheerfulness. I felt pretty good while at the same time I knew I shouldn't.

While I was making coffee for us I noticed Maura's eyes flicking in my direction and then lingering. Not in any sexual way. She was keeping tabs on me and she didn't want me to know. I was tempted to tell her I was all right, because I was pretty sure I was. But I had this inclination to keep quiet and just let everything unfold while I watched. Maybe I would let the world come to me instead of working so hard to make it bend to my will. I placed Maura's cup on the table in front of her and sat down in my place opposite her.

"Do you want me to turn the news on?" she asked softly.

I considered that question for a couple of moments.

My mind made a weird connection between Maura's turning on her radio there in the kitchen and my clicking her computer's mouse in her study a few minutes ago. One click. Then another, to find out if the first click worked. We both sat still. The radio stayed quiet. I thought it was fine for things to stay just that way.

After a while Maura said, "It's probably not going to hit the news until later this afternoon or this evening." The volume of her voice had gone up a notch. She was studying my face. I decided that she was trying to get me to talk. Slyly testing me the way people do when somebody's been knocked out. Or waking up from anesthesia.

I'm fine, I started to say, but something in me didn't want to break my silence. It was silly, I knew, and I was a little amused at myself. Easy enough just to say yes or no. So why not say one or the other? Well, one reason was that I didn't care which it was. Listen to the radio or don't listen. I no longer felt the necessity to decide such matters.

I took a sip of my coffee and smiled at the mug as I set it back on the table. That coffee was really excellent. I was suddenly just so grateful to Maura for finding it, buying it, and bringing it here so that I could have this sip I'd just taken. I smiled at her. I was very grateful to her for sitting there with me. I gave her a great big smile, which made her cut her eyes at me, but I also saw from the way her mouth flashed a fast grin that she had decided I was okay. I probably looked like a doofus, and she probably thought I was doing it on purpose. Maybe I was.

Maura had always been pretty good at keeping quiet. Better than I was, that's for sure. So anyway, we sat at the table, and we drank our coffee. We could have been two people sitting in the middle of a vast prairie, nothing around us for miles and miles in any direction. I just kept feeling more and more uplifted. But not like when I used to smoke pot in high school and college. This updraft had a death component to it, like you hear in old hymns—"In the Sweet By and By" or "Shall We Gather by the River." Either I had already died, or I was going to die in the next minute, and either way it would be fine. From my freshman English class at Hofstra, I remembered Professor Bornhauser telling us Keats's last words were *Don't be frightened.* My life was all tidied up. I was right with the world and everybody I'd ever known. Envisioning my tombstone I almost giggled aloud: JACK PLYMOUTH—AT THE END HE GOT RIGHT WITH THE WORLD. Or maybe: JACK PLYMOUTH—HE WASN'T FRIGHTENED.

If I had felt like talking, I'd have asked Maura if she'd ever had that fantasy of thinking she had just died, maybe in a car wreck or a sniper got her, but to her consciousness it had felt like she just kept on going without even stopping or knowing that she was actually dead. I'm not sure that's what was going on with me right then, but I felt just outrageously refurbished—like I had traded in the old model of me for a brand-new one.

Maura finished her coffee, stood up, placed her cup in the sink, then reached out a hand to me. "Shall we get back on the road, Jack? Hit the road, in the good way?" She had the slightest little curl at either side of her mouth, and the thought occurred to me that maybe she, too, was feeling this upgrade of the spiritual interior. Maybe she and I were both dead and didn't know it—maybe Kira had reported us and the FBI had figured out what we'd been doing, had discovered Maura's Method, had mounted a counterattack, and had taken us out while we were in her study. Just zapped us into oblivion. I held onto her hand and met her eyes—she was not tugging on me to make me stand up, and I was not standing up of my own volition. We were both so still it was as if someone had hit the "pause" button. I didn't know where that happy little lull between us came from. Nor did I know why I placed my other hand—my left—on her knee and slid it up her thigh, underneath her skirt. Or let's just say I had no advance notice of my hand's intention. A little bird song out there on the prairie.

"Hey..." she said. But it was a very soft "hey," what I understood pretty quickly to be a colluding "hey." The weather had been warm, and so she wasn't wearing pantyhose or tights. The surface of her right inner thigh could hardly have felt more welcoming. She shifted her stance a little so as to steady herself on the table and to give my left hand some room to maneuver. While that old investigative hand made its way, taking its time—because what was the hurry if we were both dead?—she inhaled significantly. "This is new," she sighed with her exhale. "I don't think we've been here before, have we, Jack?"

Her voice stayed soft enough to clue me in that her question was rhetorical. *It's new, all right*, I was inclined to say, but I didn't have to. This was the thing with Maura right now, this was what we had been moving toward all along, and maybe we both had to be dead before it could happen like that—she knew what had happened and where we were. Prairie of the interior life. She knew so well that I could set aside talking or speaking aloud. I needed both hands to lift her skirt properly, and she helped with that, helped, too, with the sliding down of her underpants—that's what she called them, she had explained to me some time ago. She told me that the word *panties* always struck her as titillating. We must have struck a silent bargain then to use *underpants* as the word for what we both worked with some urgency to untangle from around her ankles and her feet. She had very sensibly stepped out of her clogs. What I would have told her then if I had been talking was that in my brain *underpants* had just overtaken *panties* as the more salacious word. The better word altogether. We also both worked with some urgency at the zipper of my pants, the untucking of her blouse, and the loosening of the clasp of her bra. Clearly it was time for me to stand up.

"Shouldn't we just go to the bedroom?" Maura whispered into my ear as my lips and teeth commenced a rediscovery and reacquaintance project with her breasts. Her body seemed to like staying right where we were. Bird song and wildflowers. I considered asking her if her nipples had always been this sturdy and willing, but just as it was perfectly evident that neither of us wished to go to the bedroom, it was also obvious to me that questioning a nipple's enthusiasm would be really dumb. And who would try to carry on a conversation anyway, with a damn table squeaking like it was about to break itself into kindling? Not that we didn't make some noises ourselves. I may not have been speaking aloud but the rules didn't say anything about panting, grunting, or snorting. It was like a language I had learned for the occasion, and Maura seemed to know it just as well as I did. This was not just new, this was God-damned revolutionary!

⌘

Okay, so we suffered some minor injuries. When one leg of the table gave way, it dumped us onto the floor, not quite a fall but definitely a quick and spontaneous readjustment of our positioning. We ended up with me flat out on the floor, arms flapped out Jesus style, and Maura leaning against the dishwasher with her legs straight out in front of her like Raggedy Ann. We were both panting hard and laughing even though I saw some blood on my hand. I wasn't sure if it was mine or hers, and she was just then realizing that she must have banged her right elbow pretty hard, because it was hurting enough to twist her face up into a grimace and make her rub it hard with her left hand.

"Lord have mercy," she said out of some mixture of pain, amusement, and astonishment. "What the hell was that?" she asked.

I made a little waggling gesture with my hand and grinned at her. It wasn't quite my doofus grin, but it made her smile. I started touching my face and neck with my fingers to see if I could find out where I was bleeding.

"Right here," she said, touching just below her collarbone and pointing at the same place on me. "I'm sorry," she said. She looked at her fingernails. "I had no idea."

⌘

We were back on the road, taking the exit off I-66 down toward Warrenton. I'd wondered if I'd have to start talking again when we got back in the car, but so far it hadn't been necessary. Though she hadn't said anything about it—or even seemed to notice it all that much—Maura must have been cooperating with me in my phase of going wordless. She didn't ask me direct questions then wait for me to answer, the way we ordinarily conversed. When she did propose a question, she caught herself and started answering it herself before I began to speak. And sometimes her answers were stunningly accurate versions of the answers I'd have given if I were speaking. This demonstrated a couple of things—that even though we'd been together only a few months she had come to know me much better than I'd realized, and that she could sustain our conversations for quite a long time without my even saying a word. It was nice, really, no longer feeling the need to say anything because my companion didn't need me to—sort of like getting out of the city and into the green countryside. Springtime on the prairie.

I was driving again, which brought me to thinking that a man behind the steering wheel of a Mercedes should have the option of speaking or not speaking, as he pleases. We were headed for Charlottesville this time, a good town to spend the night in before we headed up onto the Skyline Drive. I decided that if I broke my silence any time soon, I'd suggest a visit to Monticello. Maybe the great articulator of the three self-evident truths would have some guidance to offer Maura and me. She and I might do just fine if he could pass along to us just one very sturdy self-evident truth.

Maura was DJ-ing on her iPod again. She started out with some of Bruce's old Jersey Shore tunes—"Sandy" and "Independence Day" and "Jersey Girl"—but then she found "Mansion on the Hill," where Bruce and his wife do this transcendent a capella semi-yodel break. Something about just the two of them blending their voices took hold of me in my silence—a man and a woman, crooning by themselves up into the night like wolves but in front of thousands of people in an outdoor stadium. Maura played it twice and it made her cry softly both times, so now she started playing other duets, like Meatloaf and Ellen Foley's "Paradise by the Dashboard Light" and some great old Nanci Griffith and Emmylou Harris pieces like "This Old House by the Road" and "Boulder to Birmingham" and "In My Hour of Darkness."

All those two-person songs playing while we made our way down through the central Virginia countryside had an effect on Maura. While the Mercedes transported us through that geography—and she must have been working on an interior journey—she gradually moved her body closer and closer to mine. We didn't have more than a few inches to work with, but even though the console was adamant about separating us, she and I managed to make our shoulders touch, she had her hand on my knee, and she was talking to me almost as if a voice had come up in her that enabled her to communicate with my interior state.

They say grieving if it's really intense can take the form of hysteria. It must have been that way for me for a long while after Ben died. Funny thing was, I had no idea how it had hit me. He'd had the cancer—in his shoulder, of all places!—and we'd thought that kind of cancer couldn't kill him. Plus he was young and strong as a horse—at least for a while. But then it did drag him down. He just died, and it felt like this very flat fact. What could I do with it, it was stupid as a rock, I couldn't move it, and it wouldn't go away. Ben was my brother, the closest person in my life until then or ever until maybe now. Maura paused and gave my knee just the slightest squeeze before she went on.

I felt like my mind and my heart weren't strong enough to

hurt like that—they couldn't bear it on their own, so the rest of my body pitched in to rescue me. It felt the way I imagined it would if somebody punched me really hard right in the center of my chest. I had this pain that hurt me all the time no matter what I did, awake, asleep, lying down, standing up, moving or sitting still, it just hurt. And I knew that that was how it was and that it would get better after a long time. But meanwhile it was just this flat fact—or two facts: my brother died; I hurt. I understood.

I was going to be thirteen in a week, and we were not going to have a party. My parents and I agreed on that. "Last thing we need," my father muttered when my mom told him my birthday was coming up. Even Ben agreed, a couple of weeks before it happened, when he could still talk to us. "Nah, don't have a party," he told us. "I can't be there. Wait till I get better," he said. He was fooled just like us—cancer in the shoulder—he knew it might be bad, but he was sure he'd get well.

What I didn't understand then was the hysteria part of it. I'm still not sure that's the right word. It's what you feel if half of yourself just drops off a cliff, but how often does that happen to you? You're alive, you've got your brain, your heart beats, but the half of you that gave you pleasure and joy and something to look forward to is missing, absent, not there. Even then there weren't any words that could help me. So I did crazy things that seemed to me perfectly reasonable. Or necessary. I'd stay awake as long as I could keep my eyes open. Then when it felt like I'd been asleep only a few minutes, my eyes would snap open. I'd probably slept at least an hour or two, but I felt like I'd only just blinked. So there I'd be, wide awake in the middle of the night, and instead of trying to get back to sleep, I'd just haul myself out of bed, pick some clothes up off the floor, put them on, step outside the house, and start walking. Moving my body felt the best I was able to feel, even though that wasn't particularly good. At least I was distracted, and I preferred that, especially at night when there was almost nobody out to see me. Or hear me, because of course I talked to Ben when I was out there. Told him he was a rat and a filthy dog for leaving me by myself after teaching me what it felt like to be with somebody. I'd sing him "Killing the Blues" when I was sure nobody could hear me. Sometimes I'd sing it sweet, but mostly I sang it mad. Either way it probably sounded the same. I also did a lot of crying out there. I'd lose track of when I started crying and when I stopped. It made no difference anyway. I didn't have to stop myself—there was nobody out there to see me and ask what was wrong.

My parents were taking sleeping pills, so I could have slammed doors and thrown dishes—I actually thought about doing both—and I wouldn't have awakened them. And even when they were awake it was like they were sleepwalking. Which pissed me off, even though I knew they felt bad that they couldn't do anything for me. Couldn't even do anything for themselves. I didn't realize it, but I blamed them for Ben dying. And of course I blamed Ben, too, but with him it felt like anger and forgiveness all lumped into one awful feeling. Anyway, when I got myself out there in the night it felt a little better. I liked the way the streetlights cast those crazy shadows.

Clarksville is put together in a way that makes no sense, so I could walk three blocks from our house on Porters Bluff Road and be down in the black neighborhood of Reynolds Street and Dodd Street, which is more like a back alley in a country town and which everybody thought was really scary. When I was moving through that part of town I'd see black folks sitting out on their porches or standing out on

120

the sidewalk smoking or talking. They did nothing to make me afraid of them. Sometimes they'd speak to me, and I'd speak back, like it was a normal thing for me to be out there at night. And if I didn't see anybody around, I'd sing "Sin City," that old Emmylou Harris and Gram Parsons song, because I was sure it would keep me safe no matter where I walked.

Maura put on Greg Brown's "Samson" for me and said she thought it was the toughest song she knew. She said she still sang it when she felt the need for some additional strength. And I could see what she meant, because it stirred me up in a way you wouldn't think possible for a guy in a Mercedes floating like a space ship through the twilit Virginia countryside. I got hit with a convergence of Maura's having spoken to me at such length, Greg Brown's channeling Samson—telling how many were dead and what he wanted to do to the old building—and the Mercedes serving me so effortlessly it was like God was letting me borrow His own limousine. I nearly swooned with another jolt of very steep uplift that felt like one of those carnival rides that haul you up into the air so fast it takes your breath away. The world was having its way with me.

Maura was beside me, very close. "Jack, put your hands back on the steering wheel," she said. Feather soft. "Please," she said, and she moved her hand on my knee ever so slightly. Not as if she was going to take the wheel, but as if she wanted me to take it. The whole time I had us floating in the divine slipstream she kept that hand on my knee and the other one on her knee. Maybe she had already received her interior adjustment and all that time

I'd been kind of hanging onto her skirt. Maybe the two of us had been soaring through crazyland for the past five or six months. Which felt fine to me. The assassination duo. The stealth eliminators. "Jack," Maura said. "Please," she said. "Your hands."

⌘

We were staying at the English Inn. It was all we could find that wasn't a chain. Maura was teaching me Hatred of Chains as a way to a better life. The architecture of this place was Tudor slapdash and retro quaint inside, with coats of arms hung on every available wall. At the desk we had to deal with a condescending old duffer with a faux accent and a blazer and red plaid tie. He made us wait while he called housekeeping to be certain that our room had been completely "prepared" for us. He might have been the owner; he might have been a homeless guy they dressed up to play the role of a supercilious Brit. In any case, Maura turned to me and rolled her eyes back toward him. In my current state of mind I thought about leaning across the desk and straightening his tie for him. "A gold-plated door," I wanted to tell him, "won't keep out the Lord's burning rain." But I was still not talking, and of course it would have been hard to convey that thought without getting verbal.

"Not half bad, eh, mate?" Maura said as we entered the room. I snorted in agreement. Maybe I was on the way back to talking. Or maybe snorting met the approval of whatever cat it was that had gotten my tongue. In my opinion, a snort was all that half-decent room merited. I wanted to say I'd prefer to sleep in the Mercedes, but I knew Maura would think that was capricious. She'd worry about me.

She announced that she was starved and set forth with her computer and her phone to find us a restaurant and make a reservation. Then she accomplished what I could only consider a miracle of time and transportation—she swept us out of the room, out of the English Inn, out to the Mercedes, which she drove downtown to a perfect parking place around the corner from Hamilton's at First and Main. Then very cozily, her arm in mine, she walked me from the car and into the restaurant where almost instantly we were seated at a great table off to the side and slightly protected from the eyes of the other diners. "I'll order for you," she said. I reached for her hand and kissed it. She could see that I was so grateful to her for taking care of me—and for the dear expression on her face—that I was even a little teary-eyed.

SAY UNCLE

As if she'd been hiding underneath the table, Kira suddenly occupied the chair across the table from me. She was just there! Her face was flushed as if she was excited to surprise us. I stood up so abruptly that I knocked my chair over behind me. Maura, too, was startled enough to set down the water glass from which she'd been about to sip. Kira gave us a radiant smile and a tinny-bright hello that were more than a little disturbing. She was herself, but there was something severely altered about her. She could have been a digital version of the Kira that Maura and I last saw sunning herself on the beach. Now in a shimmering red silk blouse with an overstated gold necklace and matching earrings, she looked right for a Palm Beach cocktail party but very peculiar in a college town restaurant on a weeknight. Even in that fancy evening outfit, she looked so youthful I doubted she would be able to persuade our waiter to bring her wine or a cocktail.

Then a gentleman stepped forward and stood a foot or so behind our table's fourth chair, his hands held loosely at his sides. He appeared to be taking care not to seem aggressive. He was wearing an elegant dark suit, white shirt, and a gray tie with a barely visible diagonal stripe in it. "May I join you please?" he asked, his voice low and ingratiating. Though he didn't smile, his expression was pleasant enough.

I nodded to signal, *Of course*, while Maura spoke for both of us. "Yes, yes, please do." Her social voice in this situation was one I hadn't heard before. Her face looked tense, as if she was determined to be mannerly.

"I hope we're not intruding," the gentleman said, now allowing himself a restrained smile. He glanced politely back and forth between Maura and me, checking to be certain we were giving him permission to sit down with us. His accent was definitely American but not one that I associated with any particular region. He was more or less my age, in his mid-forties, maybe even fifty, but unlike me he was movie-star handsome—think of George Clooney, or generations ago Clark Gable or Gregory Peck. Nothing doofus about this fellow.

"My Uncle Jimmy," Kira said with a little gesture as the man very carefully took his seat. When Maura shook hands with Uncle Jimmy, she told him her first name and mine. I reached across the table to shake his hand. In our conversation with Kira on the beach those weeks ago we had told her our first names, but I was pretty certain we'd never given her our last names—or any information that would have allowed her to track us down. So it was eerie to see her there, looking like yet another variation of the Kira Gregorevna we knew as Dr. Hatemo's personal assistant. Even though she was radically changed, I didn't have any doubt that it was the same person. I still had no impulse to talk, though I suspected I might have to speak before we parted company with Kira and her uncle.

Maura quickly asked, "What brought you to Charlottesville, Uncle Jimmy?"

The elegant man nodded modestly to acknowledge Maura's calling him exactly what Kira had called him. He was one of those fellows whose confidence was so complete that he really should have been in an old black-and-white movie with somebody like Audrey Hepburn. He even had the neatly barbered salt-and-pepper hair that would make him right for the role. I half expected him to pull out a silver case and offer cigarettes around the table.

Uncle Jimmy explained that he was here for a conference of Jefferson scholars from around the world. He told us that while the scholars could not actually hold their meetings at Monticello, they had been allowed special access to the estate and to the documents and materials that were located there. His face became quite animated while he spoke of his academic colleagues. "You would think that the newly revealed and much-discussed flaws of the great man would have diminished scholarly interest in him. In fact the opposite is the case. Political scientists from China and Russia are obsessed with the question of how the person who penned the phrase 'all men are created equal' could not during his lifetime give his slaves their freedom."

Uncle Jimmy sighed and checked our faces before he went on. "The facts that interest these rarefied folks the most are Jefferson's fathering children with Sally Hemings and her remaining his slave until he died. What scholars of all varieties understand about each other is that ultimately they want to talk about scandals, although they prefer to do it under the pretense of discussing matters of the intellect. To be frank, I think their primary reason for attending this conference is that they wanted to walk around in the rooms where Jefferson and Sally Hemings conceived their children. Breathe that air. Feel those floors beneath their own feet." Uncle Jimmy paused before saying softly, almost as if confessing his own transgression, "I saw one of the ladies, a highly revered biographer from Cambridge, brushing her fingertips over the slip cover on that alcove bed when the tour guide wasn't looking." He pursed his lips in sad bemusement.

Uncle Jimmy unfurled a most engaging personality while he spoke. It was pretty obvious that he was putting on a little show for us. With his twinkling eyes that met ours as he talked and his deep authoritative voice, he charmed away much of the anxiety that Maura and I felt about the situation. I could not, however, discern what Kira thought about the raconteur mode the man she'd introduced as her relative seemed to have taken on for our sake. I glanced at her often enough to notice that her facial expression remained rigidly pleasant and that her eyes flicked again and again toward Uncle Jimmy's hands, which were pale and large but shapely as a pianist's and nicely manicured. I, too, began sneaking looks in that direction, because now that I had noticed those hands they appeared to be enacting a little performance to complement Uncle Jimmy's remarks. His fingers made restrained movements that accompanied his sentences. "One might suspect that the narrative of Jefferson and Hemings at Monticello is a scholarly manifestation of pornography," he said with a chuckle and a slow drum roll of his fingers on the tablecloth.

When our waiter approached, after Maura had ordered for the two of us, Uncle Jimmy ordered dinner for both Kira and himself. For their drinks he ordered ginger ale for her, and for himself he asked for Stolichnaya elit, neat. He did so without consulting Kira and without any change in her demeanor. I glanced at Maura to see how she was responding, then immediately chided myself. Did I really need her to guide me in understanding what was up with Uncle Jimmy and Kira? But then I had to admit that the peculiar dynamic between those two was beyond me. I did need help with it, and I would not have looked to anyone but Maura for such help. She and I had moved out to our own special province of interpreting human intercourse.

Suddenly Kira stirred herself and began speaking with gestures and bright energy—she was almost the Kira of Palm Beach again. "Maura and Jack, when I saw you two people here in the restaurant, I pointed you out to Uncle Jimmy and reminded him that I had mentioned you before. More than a few times. Because I so much enjoyed talking with you. He told me he hoped that I would ask you to accompany us to our suite in the hotel. He has a question he would like to ask you." Kira's face and her voice were very, very friendly.

But the name of what entered my consciousness right then—wondering what Uncle Jimmy's question might be—was fear. I also suspected him of having given Kira a tap on the shin with the toe of his shoe to signal her to speak up as she did. But I counseled myself—*are we not in a restaurant filled with well-to-do people in a college town?* And had not Uncle Jimmy shown himself to be a cultivated man, a scholar with good manners and a sense of humor?

"We're staying at the Omni. Just across the street and up the hill a few steps. It's quite a hotel—for a town like Charlottesville." Uncle Jimmy looked to my face, then to

Maura's, to gauge, I suppose, our feelings about hotels. Or more likely, our feelings about paying a visit to his and Kira's suite in the Omni.

"Kira and I shopped for chocolates today." He beamed an indulgent grin in her direction. "She would love to share with you some of the treasures we found. And I have some brandy." Now his eyes suggested that he was pleading with us. "She tells me that she had an inspiring conversation with you some weeks ago," he said, nodding. "She tells me that you are both quite accomplished people." He opened his hands to us and smiled. "Please," he said.

Maura nodded. I did, too. I didn't really know why we couldn't refuse Uncle Jimmy's offer, and I doubted that Maura knew either. I did know that neither of us wanted to go to their room in the Omni. And I did know that we were going to do it. Maybe it was his *please* that persuaded us. We might be out in our own special province, but we were still vulnerable to a sincere-sounding *please*. But if he did ask us what we intended to do with the information Kira had given us, then what would our answer be?

⌘

Even in the elevator I had a flash of believing it was still possible for us to say that we'd changed our minds. I noticed Kira's hand trembling when she extracted the card for their room from her purse. The four of us had remained silent all the way to the top floor. I realized that Maura hadn't seen Kira's unsteady hand and that if we were to excuse ourselves from the visit, it would be up to me to voice it. I stayed quiet.

The three of us stood outside Uncle Jimmy's suite in grave silence watching Kira swipe the card through the slot to unlock the door—she did it quickly so that I couldn't see if her hand was still unsteady. I realized, too, that I'd managed to go this far through the evening without actually uttering words or sentences, though I had grunted and hummed, nodded, smacked my lips, shaded my eyes with my hands, tilted my head, and tsk-tsked. I might have been a virtuoso of wordless communication, but I berated myself on all other counts—a foolish, spineless, stupidly voiceless and cowardly assassin was what I was. Even then, when I could have spoken so easily—*I'm sorry, Kira and Uncle Jimmy, I'm not feeling so well, I'm afraid I need Maura to drive me back to our hotel, please forgive us*—I didn't.

"When Kira's employer transitioned," Uncle Jimmy was telling us as we entered the room—I reminded myself to remember that 507 was the number. He paused to close the door behind us. "When we learned of his passing, of course we members of Kira's family knew that we had to reach out to offer her our help."

"What did you call it?" Maura asked him with some tension in her voice. Her face suggested insult or mild horror rather than curiosity. "Did you just say, 'transitioned'?"

Uncle Jimmy chuckled politely. "Yes," he said. "It's a way they have of speaking of it in Florida nowadays. Perhaps because there are so many folks down there who are on the verge of *transitioning*." He spoke directly to Maura to signal his appreciation of her noting the word. "That's where I first heard it," he said. "When I flew down there to pick up Kira. But I also wonder if it might have been coined by someone like Steven Colbert or one of the writers for *Saturday Night Live*. People in Palm Beach use it frequently and cheerfully, albeit with very little irony. In New Jersey we still say, 'croaked' or 'checked out' or 'bought the farm,' and we use those terms with the usual droll tongue in cheek. My colleagues at the university enjoy saying, 'graduated.' They're very cheerful because they're around young people all the time."

Maura said, "Ha!" and glanced meaningfully at me. I blinked at her. I had nothing to offer. I didn't really know what to make of what he'd said. In that room through which a thousand strangers must have passed, the best I could hope for was an hour or so of profoundly boring chit-chat.

Uncle Jimmy removed his suit jacket, loosened his tie, and with a soft murmur and a gesture toward the bar directed Kira to bring out the chocolates. "Please," he said to Maura and me. "Sit down. Make yourselves comfortable." He gestured toward the sofa while taking the big leather easy chair across from us. "Maura," he said. "Jack," he said. He nodded and smiled benignly. He seemed so fond of us he could have been our own uncle, entertaining us lavishly in his fancy hotel room. He unbuttoned his starched cuffs and rolled them up. Then he opened the drawer of the table beside the chair and removed from it a small black handgun and a black tube, which he screwed onto the barrel end of the weapon. He did that with aplomb, clearly enjoying the act of joining the two parts, the sudden intensity with which Maura and I watched him, and the heft of the thing in his hand. He looked it over with evident admiration, touched something on it that made a quiet snap, then gingerly set it on the table beside him. I was relieved to see that the extended barrel was not pointed toward Maura or me. "One can never be too careful," he said amiably. "I'm sure you know that. Even in Charlottesville," he said.

I felt Maura shift on the sofa beside me. If there is a noise a person makes when she shrinks into herself as much as she possibly can, that would have been what I heard from her direction. Which is to say that even though there was no sound that came from her, I nevertheless heard the very compressed silence into which she fell.

As for me, my mind stayed floaty, functioning as if it had finally come loose from whatever tethers of responsibility had held it in place through all my years. Ever since my single-click moment in Maura's study, it had been that way. So my response to Uncle Jimmy's pistol was irritatingly detached. *I wonder how he will use it*, was my first thought. I played through a fast scenario of his shooting Maura and me in his hotel suite, bloodying up the sofa and the carpet even if the weapon didn't make much noise. I concluded that he was not likely to do something that crude. Even so, imagining Uncle Jimmy's leveling the gun, first at me, then at Maura, should have been more disturbing than it was. I couldn't seem to take it in, to make it real in my mind. But then he hadn't done anything directly threatening yet. He had merely brought his pistol out into the open, attached a silencer to it, and set it aside. Like a toy he wanted us to see. I told myself that Uncle Jimmy could just be a gun enthusiast. And immediately imagined Maura's "Ha!" in response to that idea. I felt as if I was both watching and acting in a very tense scene in a movie. My moronic brain was whispering to me, *How do you think this is going to turn out? Will you leave this room alive?*

Kira brought the chocolates. I saw her take note of the pistol on the table with a quick glance. Her expressionless face made me think of fossils, mummies, primitive masks. She stood to the side of Uncle Jimmy's firing lanes, half-way between him and Maura and me. She kept her face directed toward him.

"Offer your treats to your friends," Uncle Jimmy directed her. Were it not for the weapon on the table, we would have taken his voice and demeanor to be perfectly sociable.

Without letting her eyes meet ours, Kira bent to offer the box of chocolates. Maura selected one, then I did, too, all the while thinking *How odd! How astonishingly odd!* Not only did I accept a chocolate, I also accepted an available peek down Kira's blouse while she bent to offer the candy. Her bra was red, and that fact, in its logic and ordinariness, somehow pleased me. *Good for you, Kira,* I thought. *A proper bra for this occasion.*

Then she stepped across the carpet to extend the box toward Uncle Jimmy. I'd been suspecting this all along but it was in that moment that I knew it for sure: He's about as much her uncle as that weapon is a water pistol.

"Thank you, my dear," he murmured to her as he selected his chocolate. "And why don't you make yourself comfortable right here," he said, patting the arm of his easy chair—the one opposite the table where the handgun rested. "Dear Kira," he said. He took a bite of his chocolate and gestured toward us. "Please," he said. "Delicious," he said, nodding in our direction.

Maura and I, like marionettes, lifted our chocolates to our mouths.

"So," he said. "Kira," he said, smiling toward us. He

set his left hand on her thigh. "My little Kira tells me that you are journalists, yes? She says that she told you all about herself, yes?"

If I had been speaking I would have attempted to talk Uncle Jimmy away from the notion that Maura and I might expose him somehow with our journalistic endeavors. Of course I would have to begin by explaining to him that actually I made my living buying and selling stock, and I'd have to hope that in the course of my explanation, I could invent a credible excuse for why Maura and I had allowed Kira to believe that we were freelance writers working on a story about "The Real Palm Beach." The human brain, even a recently untethered one like mine, is a marvelous instrument. In a split second of reviewing possible stories I might try to tell Uncle Jimmy, I raced to the conclusion that it was a very good thing that I wasn't talking.

"Yes," Maura said. Very calmly. "Yes, that's right."

"My question for you then," Uncle Jimmy said, leaning forward, touching his fingertips together to make a little cage in front of himself, "is what do you plan to do with the information you obtained from your interview with my niece?"

Maura and I were both quiet for some moments during which Uncle Jimmy looked quizzically from one to the other of us. I was aware of my imbecile brain's just closing up, flattening out, as if it was switching itself into emergency mode, disabling itself, generating no thought.

"We haven't written up the story yet," Maura said. Her voice shocked me. She could have been conversing with an editor or an agent. She had uttered a very sensible response to Uncle Jimmy's question. "We haven't yet gotten a commitment from a magazine," she told him. She was doing her best to turn the interrogation into a professional discussion.

Uncle Jimmy nodded. "My little Kira—Perhaps I should say '*our* little Kira' now, because when you obtained that information from her, you—how should I put it?—*invested* in her. My advice to you," he said, giving me a nod and a smile, almost as if he thought I needed encouragement, "is that you bear in mind the harm you might bring to this little one with your story." He paused to look at Maura and me to be sure we were paying attention. "Of course I don't know exactly what she told you, but I am concerned because our little Kira is very young, you know? Well, you may not know, because she has an extraordinary history." He shifted in his chair to look up at the girl's face, which was slightly above his. She did not meet his look; instead she inclined her head forward as if to study the carpet. Her hair fell forward around her face. "Haven't you, little Kira?" His voice was very soft.

I wasn't sure how he managed this, but in an instant, leaning forward but still remaining seated, Uncle Jimmy had grabbed a handful of Kira's hair with his left hand, had stood her up and twisted her around, so that now she was kneeling directly in front him with her back to us. Kira herself was silent and amazingly pliable in the way she had allowed him to force her up, twist her around, and then yank her downward. It was as if the two of them were gymnasts who had rehearsed these moves. "Haven't you had a very special history, Kira?" Uncle's Jimmy's voice had taken on some timbre. He'd held onto Kira's hair. Now he gave her head a shake at the same time he pulled her forward and closer to him. "Tell your friends, please," he says.

"Yes." Her voice was barely audible, muffled as it was by her having her back to us and her mouth being directed more or less toward Uncle Jimmy's belt buckle. He shook her head again. "I have very much history," she said. Her voice was louder, but it was still partially stifled.

"Let's show your friends what you've learned in your brief life, my dear. Let's show them how you know what needs to happen in a situation like this." Uncle Jimmy was looking down at Kira's blond hair, but the instant Maura started to stand he placed his right hand exactly beside the pistol on the table.

"Maura, do you know the military term 'order of battle'?" he asked. His eyes flashed at her, but his voice was as genial as if he were teaching a graduate seminar. "'Order of battle' has to do with planning the sequence of what will happen when one military unit is about to engage another military unit."

Maura straightened to a standing position, but she didn't step forward. Though his eyes were focused on her, Uncle Jimmy didn't move his right hand.

"Should you have engagement in mind, Maura, you should consider how I am likely to respond. Let me tell you why I think you should sit down. If you take a single step forward, I will first shoot Jack. Probably with that first shot I will not kill him, but I can assure you that he will be what people in your line of business call 'fatally injured.' He will be unable to help you. Then my second act will be to bring the butt of this weapon" —he nodded toward the table— "down very hard against our Kira's head. Right here," he said, moving aside a lock of Kira's hair with his left hand to expose a swatch of pale skin behind her ear. That pinkish white area at the base of her skull terrified me even in my emotionally paralyzed state.

Uncle Jimmy continued, but his voice was softer now. "Those actions will occur in the time it takes for you to move from where you stand now to where I sit here. Then you will be very close, and I will have the weapon in my hand. So then we will see how it goes with you." He paused several moments while he continued watching Maura. Somehow he managed to keep a civilized expression on his face. "It could be very interesting," he said. "How it goes with you—when Jack and Kira are no longer part of the 'order of battle.'" He paused again. "But perhaps you can see why I think sitting down is your best course of action right now," he said.

"Can we please just go?" Maura whispered to him. "I promise you we..."

"No, Maura," Uncle Jimmy said. He shook his head in the manner of a parent who must say no to a daughter for her own good. "Your education is not complete. A little piece of knowledge you still need," he said. "For your journalism," he said. "Sit down."

Maura sat. I felt heat emanating from her. She was on the verge of bursting into flames.

"Now, Kira, please go ahead. While your friends are making themselves comfortable."

Kira's arms lifted her hands toward Uncle Jimmy's pants in front of her. I was very glad I couldn't see her face.

"You see, Maura and Jack, what you are about to learn is how a person can stay alive when she has accepted the fact that she is utterly disposable." He paused and shifted in his chair to accommodate Kira's mission with his pants, but he kept his eyes on us. It occurred to me that he was actually still being professorial. He was committing a pedagogical act. That I could even come up with such a thought nauseated me. Then a voice from somewhere else in me called from so far away that I hardly recognized it. *Better that all three of you should die than for you to sit and allow this to happen.* I doubted that I had it in me even to reach a standing position. Nevertheless I felt my body gathering itself.

"Like so much tissue paper," Uncle Jimmy said to us through his teeth. "That is what Kira knows," he said.

I focused my eyes above his head.

Maura fumbled for my hand, found it, and held on very tightly.

"Yes, Maura. A human being can be wadded up and thrown away," he said. His eyes were hooded then, but they were not closed, we could see that. "Waste," he said.

NIGHT JOURNEY

Shining like a miracle under the streetlights, the Mercedes was parked where we had left it—not that there was any reason why it shouldn't have been. Because we had been shaking hard, Maura and I had navigated the whole way back there clutching each other so tightly we might have been mistaken for Siamese twins. It was late, though, and the few people out at that hour had little interest in a couple walking wrapped up in each other's arms. We had kept our eyes only on the sidewalk in front of us, and we had walked as crisply as we could, given that our footsteps had to be synchronized. Now, braced against the car, we faced each other and held on even tighter. I felt what she felt, and we were both trembling inside and out. Holding on had gotten us that far—now we were afraid of what might happen if we let go. Against my chest I felt her teeth chattering and maybe some wetness seeping through my shirt—I couldn't tell if it was tears, snot, or sweat. When she pressed the keys into my hand, I walked her around to the passenger side, unlocked the door, held it for her, then hurried around to the driver's side and climbed in.

I started the car, locked the doors, turned to stare at Maura. The streetlight showed me her face, which was a mess. "Of course he could still shoot us," I said quietly. It was a shock to hear myself utter words again, not to mention a complete sentence. But it made me feel restored— I hadn't quite realized what a box I was in without my words.

Maura nodded and made a noise that sounded like whale song. She contorted herself to swing her legs across the console and into my lap. Her face pleaded with me. I knew she wanted me to hold her legs or her knees or something like that. I was more than happy to do so—I, too, felt compelled to touch her, to connect our bodies, as if physical contact would somehow correct the awful thing we had just lived through.

"Shooting us in the car would actually make a lot more sense than shooting us in the hotel room," I said. It was kind of thrilling to have reclaimed possession of language. It occurred to me that even though I was probably still in danger of being murdered by Kira's evil "family," I could nevertheless say anything, anything at all. True, crazy, or stupid, I could say it. "Walk by with that pistol in his coat pocket, stop just long enough to pump a couple of rounds through the side window, and then keep walking."

Maura's face contorted, her mouth opened, and she made another of those underwater moaning sounds. She bent forward to move her face nearer mine.

"Yes, all right," I said. "You're probably right. He didn't want to kill us—too much mess, too much risk at calling attention to himself."

She shivered and shut her eyes, really squeezed her eyes shut. I stared at her and began to know what had taken hold of her. "Kira?" I murmured.

Maura opened her eyes, and I kept studying her face. She shook her head very slowly.

"All right," I said. Then it hit me hard when I got it. I was an oaf not to have understood the minute Uncle Jimmy pulled that pistol out of the drawer. Or at least the instant he grabbed Kira by the hair. "Oh, God," I said. "We really completely screwed things up for her, didn't we?"

By contorting herself severely Maura managed to press her cheekbone right up against mine. It was what I wanted, too. Her skin my skin. And who gave a good God damn whose tears these were? I hadn't been able to think of Kira as a real-life human being until that moment—first she was Hatemo's live-in fantasy servant, then she was Uncle Jimmy's girl-puppet. But all along, Maura had been holding Kira in her mind as a person—a human being struggling hard against brute nastiness that aimed to...

"You know what's too bad?" I said when Maura finally moved away and swung her legs back around to her own side of the console. "What's a really miserable piss-poor fact is that we can't..." The obvious word wasn't adequate to say aloud, and I struggled for a better one. All of a sudden I broke out laughing before I even knew what I was doing. "What really sucks is that right now from right here in the car we can't transition that motherfucker!"

I hadn't thought she would, but Maura smiled, too. She made another sea-creature noise, and I understood what she meant by it. We'd gotten that word *transition* stuck in our brains. *Transition Uncle Jimmy again and again. Bring him back to life and then slam him back down into death so many times we finally get him all the way down into the epicenter of hell.* That's what she meant.

I put the Mercedes in gear and headed out of town, aa fast as I thought I could get away with. Maura twisted the GPS around toward her so she could tell it to guide us back to DC. She completely agreed with me that we were not going back to the English Inn—at least not that night. We didn't want to allow Uncle Jimmy a single minute more of life that we could deny him.

It was when we were cruising north on Route 29 almost to Culpepper that I thought of a problem. "How are we going to ID the bastard? We might know more or less where he is, but we don't have the slightest clue what his name is or what records to access to find some data on him."

Maura pulled some little object out of her coat pocket and held it up for me to see. I was driving as much over the speed limit as I could, and the light was dim in the car anyway. So I had to glance over at the object several times while keeping my eyes mostly on the road. Finally I made it out to be a safety razor. She must have had a premonition and taken it when she went to the bathroom when we first stepped into Uncle Jimmy's suite. So, yes, it probably had exactly what she needed in the way of DNA from shaved-off whiskers and skin particles. "I still don't see…"

She held up the razor so I could see it and in the crazy light of the Mercedes interior swiped the palm of her other hand slowly an inch or so back and forth above it.

It took me a minute to process that motion of her hand into understanding: She meant she had a scanner. But even then her study wasn't set up as any kind of lab. I told her that.

She shrugged and patted my knee.

So I knew she could do it. Extract from that razor the

information she needed to locate old Uncle Jimmy and send him his own personalized death ray. "All right," I said. "I should never have doubted your powers."

Maura nodded and patted my knee again. I decided that the woman whose hand stayed resting on my knee was very likely the most ingenious executioner in the history of the world.

She gave me a look that seemed to me infused with both joy and sorrow. I knew what she meant. She must have been feeling like she'd happily give up her powers if doing so would help Kira.

"Just don't tell me that anybody can do what you do," I said. "That the secret is out there where anybody can find it," I said. "You're the only one," I told her.

She shrugged, then moved over against her door. It was a move that let me know I'd gone too far. She wasn't denying what I'd said, I understood that. But I also understood that putting it into words as I'd just done made her feel forlorn. There was no comfort for her in knowing that she alone was the master murderer of the planet. Which was why she had needed me in the first place. It occurred to me that maybe she had known all along that I could never be her equal. She had taken me anyway.

⌘

A night drive with some decent music can go a long way toward fixing what's broken in your life. When things went really bad with Vicki and me I had listened to Cat Stevens's "Peace Train" and Simon and Garfunkel's "Bridge Over Troubled Waters" until I wore them out and the songs themselves started sounding tired. Paul Simon's

Graceland album had gotten me through my divorce and giving up custody of my kids. I'd felt like the pieces of my life were falling all around me, but by God I could still hear me some music. Which is to say, I could still bring some passion to my listening. I could also get myself all cried out and feel like another life might be possible for me if I didn't kill myself or do something that landed me in jail.

Right then Maura was huddled over to herself on the far side of the car, which gave me the feeling that I was probably on my own for the rest of the drive. My companion-navigator was taking a break. Meanwhile the sound system was still moving through her Springsteen playlist. I was okay with that. I liked hearing Bruce sing and talk about his dad in "Independence Day" and "Growing Up," and he and the quiet car moving through the darkness took me right down to a place I mostly avoided going in those days—thinking about my long-dead father. Uncle Jimmy and his handgun must have shaken loose my old inclination to brood about my old man when time stretched out in front of me. It went without saying that my father wouldn't have been able to deal with the stealth murders Maura and I had committed during the past months. He wouldn't have known what to make of Maura at all. It occurred to me that if he were still alive, I wouldn't even have had the nerve to enter into this pact with Maura in the first place. I'd have figured he'd somehow find out even if I never told him.

My father was a quiet, dutiful man with a thoughtful demeanor. Because of rheumatic fever he hadn't finished college, but he had read widely and randomly, and his way of speaking was that of an educated person. Because he was a good listener, the men who worked for him at the carbide plant and the people in town often sought his counsel. From my earliest memories I had liked being in his vicinity, so I hung around and eavesdropped on those conversations. My father didn't mind, and the visitor hardly ever paid any attention to me. I was pretty good at keeping a certain distance and being unobtrusive.

The visits usually took place out in our driveway in the early evening. Around the time our family was finishing supper, a car would drive up and stop in the driveway between the house and the garage. If no one came to the door, my father would step out through the screen door with me close enough behind him that the door would slap shut only once. It would always be a man—if a woman wanted to talk to him, she'd catch him down at the post office or even come to his office at the carbide plant. So if somebody drove up to our house, it was sure to be a man and probably somebody who worked for him. He and the visitor would stand or pace near the cooling car, sometimes leaning against it or braced on one leg with a foot up on the car's bumper. I would try to locate myself in just the right place so as to be near my father—and to hear every word they spoke—but not to attract attention. From my careful listening, I understood that my father was reluctant to advise these men. To delay having to deliver an opinion, my father would question the visitor at some length—and those were the best parts of the visits, because the answers the men gave were often passionate and shocking.

Eventually the man would stop talking and wait for my father to speak his mind about the problem the man had presented. My father would shift his feet and look down at the gravel as if it were a puzzle he was struggling to solve. The man would ask, "What do you think, Mr. Plymouth—should I kick her out?" And my father would say something like, "Tell me again how many years you've been together," and the man would tell him. My father would then say something like, "Well, there's your answer, Leon. Do you kick somebody out after you've lived with her for seventeen years?" There'd be a long silence, then the man would say, "Well, I thank you, Mr. Plymouth, for hearing me out." And my father would say, "No trouble, Leon. Glad to talk to you. You take care now."

I've never been able to figure out exactly how I came to believe my father thought of killing himself pretty much all the time. I had some evidence but not much, and certainly nothing conclusive. I thought, with very little proof, that my father always worried that his place in the world was precarious and that he saw himself skating on the edge of humiliation for most of his adult life.

Like much of what I knew about my father, the idea (or opinion or suspicion or whatever it was) that my father was death-haunted had been in my mind for most of my life. That was a non-fact that resided alongside the facts that my father smoked, that on winter days when he came home from work my father usually drank a hot toddy, that on Saturday afternoons my father took a bath, and that when my father worked crossword puzzles at his desk he breathed through his mouth so that it sounded like a faintly tuneless whistling. I'd known then, as I knew now, that my father loved me and my sister and our mother. Of that I never had any doubt, or my childhood would have been much more anxious than it actually was.

I thought that as a teenager my father had probably thought about turning a gun on himself, but then I also knew my father seemed to enjoy painting by the numbers, kits that came in boxes with pictures on the front of what the finished painting would look like—blue jays in a tree, a horse in a field, a house with a blue stream of water running beside it.

There in the Mercedes floating north through the dark, I shook my head with the sudden revelation that in my childhood I had mushed together all the things I knew—or thought I knew—about him! *My father thought about death while he sat at his desk painting by the numbers and breathing through his mouth so it sounded like whistling.* A late-night thought if there ever was one.

My awareness of my father's inclination toward suicide and my considering it an ordinary aspect of our lives back then now seemed to me immensely strange. That strangeness and Maura's willed silence in her shadowy corner of the front seat and Bruce's raspy singing all around me and the car's moving through the deep darkness of the early morning hours were—and this is stranger than all of it put together—comforting to me. Maybe it was being able to hold in mind both Maura and my father—who had never met and who would have been deeply suspicious of each other if it had been possible for them to meet—that somehow calmed me. What I was—a country child—and what I'd come to be—a transition enabler—now seemed to comfortably inhabit my mental space in the Mercedes speeding north.

My father had been an only child, the son of my admirable grandfather and the witch who was my grandmother. I knew my father to have been conflicted all his life by his devotion to both parents, the ferocious mother who wanted to control his every move, the astonishingly capable father who remained in the house with the witch only to protect the son as best he could.

In his teenage years—I imagined it to have happened when he was around fourteen—my father used my grandfather's .22 pistol to shoot three holes in the full-length mirror of my grandmother's standup wardrobe. I never saw the holes in the glass because the mirror had been replaced before I was born, but I got several looks at the holes in the wooden back of the mirrored door. The holes were where my father would have seen his own face in the glass when he fired the pistol.

My sister must have decided I needed to see the mirrored door, though I don't know how she came to know the story—I couldn't imagine our father telling it to my sister or to anyone else. But he must have. Now that I thought about their relationship, I saw that he could have told her. Something made him think it was all right to confide in her. She was three years older than I was, a very reasonable girl from early on, and I knew he talked with her often when I wasn't around. In any case, I was sure my sister was the source of my knowing that he shot up that mirror. I had a pretty firm memory of her escorting me up to view the inside of my grandmother's wardrobe, and she must have chosen a time when neither of my grandparents was likely to know what we were up to.

As for my grandmother, her behavior was so extreme that the whole family dealt with it like a monstrous joke. My grandmother exercised in the nude and well into her seventies liked to demonstrate how she could stand on her head. She ranted constantly about her hatred of Eleanor and Franklin Roosevelt, the Kennedys, and Martin Luther King. She had insisted on washing her son's hair every

Sunday after the family dinners that occurred around one in the afternoon. I grew up witnessing the dynamic of my father in the company of crazy Grandmama and sweet-tempered, long-suffering Granddad. Even if my sister or somebody hadn't told me the story about the mirror, I might have come to suspect something dark like that in my father's childhood. A boy who grew up with those parents would have to think about killing himself, wouldn't he? A boy whose mother's behavior must have made public humiliation a constant possibility?

In the house of my own boyhood a black, snub-nosed pistol lived in the top drawer of my father's dresser. Perfectly reasonable for it to be there—our family lived on a gravel road in an isolated area near a rough and lawless community. From when I was around ten, if my parents or my sister weren't around, I would move through the house as slowly and quietly as a sleepwalker to the dresser, stand there a while, then open the drawer, carefully push to the side any socks or handkerchiefs in my line of sight, and stare at the pistol. If I were certain I wasn't going to be disturbed, I would gingerly lift the weapon from the drawer, always surprised and thrilled by its weight, always aware of my heartbeat speeding up. In the greater light of the room it wasn't pure black but had a bluish tint. The copper bullet-ends of the cartridges in their chamber were visible, but it made me uneasy to look at them for long because it meant the barrel of the pistol had to be pointed more or less toward me. Years later, standing out there in the weeds beside our old abandoned house, I remembered how drawn I was to the pistol. I remembered my fear of it, my desire to see it, touch it, lift it out of the drawer.

Remembered how, when I had the house to myself, the pistol summoned me.

Something I never did—though I often wonder why I didn't—was to stand in front of the mirror in my parents' bedroom and point the pistol at my reflection. Two steps from where I stood with the pistol in my hand was the mirror. If I took those steps, there I'd be, seeing myself see myself. I could lift my arm. Point the thing at my reflected head. Maybe squint to sight down the barrel at the exact point between the eyes of the boy in the mirror. Was that how my father did it when he was fourteen? And what could have pushed my father to pull the trigger? Three times. I never even took the two steps over to face the mirror. I never even put my finger on the trigger.

If I had asked my father about it, he would have looked away, shaken his head, and tried to maneuver around the question. "I don't know, son. You don't have a lot of control over what thoughts enter your mind. Especially when you're a boy." He would have glanced at me then. "A boy thinks what he thinks—surely you know that." I would have had to see the sadness in his face.

Or, "That was so long ago I can't remember it. I know I did it, but I can't remember what I was thinking." He probably would have said that without even lifting his eyes from the newspaper. I would have been hurt by his refusing to engage with me.

One Saturday afternoon I came upon my father crying at his desk. My mother was upstairs napping, my sister was in her room talking with a friend on the phone, and the radio was playing softly in the kitchen, as it usually did throughout the day. It took me a moment to realize that my father had not heard me enter his study through the hallway door behind him—which felt strange and thrilling. So I stood still a couple of feet behind him. In another moment he took off his glasses, set them aside on his desk, and put his face in his hands. He was sobbing, but so quietly that I knew he didn't want anyone to know. I tried to think what might be troubling him. I was maybe eleven or twelve, not an age of notable sensitivity. Even so, I understood that my father would be embarrassed to know that I was seeing him in a moment of sorrow or grieving. His being so quiet about it made me think he didn't want to have to explain himself. A little tremor of panic ran through me. I was trapped.

Had I been truly considerate of my father, I would have backed out of that room immediately. Or cleared my throat to let him know I was there. But I wasn't that kind of boy. That I didn't make a noise or just quietly leave the room says everything about me in that phase of my life. The word *fixated* wasn't available to me then, but that's probably what was going on with me—I wanted something from my father, though I had no idea what it was.

So I stayed put.

After a long moment I actually felt him taking it in that I was there in the room with him. Without turning to me, he pulled his handkerchief from his back pocket, blew his nose, and swabbed at his face a bit. He stuffed the handkerchief back into his pocket, picked up his glasses, and slowly swiveled his desk chair around to face me.

The moment felt endless. Since he was sitting and I was standing, my view of him was from a slightly downward angle. His face showed he'd been crying—even behind his glasses, the skin around his eyes appeared swollen and red. So he knew that I knew. Neither of us looked away from the other. I could think of nothing to say, and evidently he couldn't either. It went on and on.

Then he reached toward me, caught my hand, squeezed it so gently that he might have been touching his newborn son for the first time. Pretty quickly he let go, swiveled his chair back to his desk, opened its middle drawer, and poked around in it as if he were looking for something. I could have stayed with him and tried to start a conversation, but I was pretty sure he didn't want me to do that. So I left and went to my room to think about what I'd witnessed.

This was as close as I could come to explaining why I believed my father was death-haunted for all the years that I knew him. If Maura and I survived and stayed together long enough, there would come a time when I offered that explanation to her. I could see her nodding that she understood. Or I could see her shaking her head that she didn't.

HANDS OFF

"Wait, Maura," I called softly. She was ahead of me on the way up the steps to her apartment door. She had stayed still almost the whole drive, but she was awake and already opening her door when I shut off the car and removed the keys from the ignition. 3:37 A.M. That's what time the clock said it was when she unlocked the door and stepped into her living room, leaving it open for me as I was trying to catch up with her. Then she was taking her coat off without breaking stride. She didn't even glance at the breakfast table with a broken leg that we had propped up temporarily before we left.

"Wait, Maura," I called again, almost in a whisper. I hadn't yet figured out my feelings, but I knew I needed to talk to her. I did seem to know what Maura's intention was at that moment. And my desire for her to slow down felt almost desperate.

In her study she switched on desk lights, her computer and its bank of boosters, and a couple of other gray modules whose function I'd never understood. Maybe it was just my having been away from that room for a while, but its array of digital machines suddenly appeared more elaborate and intimidating than I had previously noticed. Right then, I wanted to shake my whole self, body and brain, like a horse or a dog. I was disoriented, as if I had stepped in there from another lifetime.

Maura sat at her big desk with her back turned to me. Her hands began fluttering over her keyboard. I doubted she even knew I was standing close behind her. Or cared. I cleared my throat. Her fingers didn't pause. She gave no sign she'd heard me.

Startling me she spun around, her face flushed, her eyes blazing. She made no sound, but she didn't have to. Right then I could read her face like a Times Square bill-board. *Jack, what the fuck do you want?!*

The heat of her impatience made me pull out the other desk chair and sit down in order to keep myself in the room with her. My first impulse had been to back away, leave her alone. Instead I faced her and started speaking.

"I don't know, Maura. Do you think we should talk about this? I mean, it was you who said you needed to feel like we had a choice. I'm with you here—I mean, of the ones we've transitioned so far, Uncle Jimmy is the one I most want dispatched straight into the flames. But I feel like maybe this is some kind of test that fate is assigning us. Like maybe we're missing something?"

She shook her head side to side. Closed her eyes.

"I'm sorry to be such a wuss at a moment like this. I don't think you're wrong. If that man were strapped into the electric chair right here right now, I'd be the first one to step up and yank down the switch. Then stand back and watch what the juice does to him. But that's not what this is. Weren't you the one who said that for us it has to be personal? I just need a little better understanding of how it can be personal if the son of a bitch is not here. I feel like we ought to be looking him in the eyes when we click the mouse on him. It's the way we do that from inside this room that's getting to me."

She opened her eyes. There was no softening of her features, but I discerned that she appreciated hearing me say, "we do." She liked it that I had said "we" three times. *We.* I felt a little tension in my shoulders dissolve.

"I mean, I know we're going to do this. I swear to God I'm with you on it. I'm ready do the click if you want. Or we can flip a coin for it. But here's my problem. Kira had a good chance of staying free if we hadn't stepped into her life. So even though we meant no harm with that trip to Florida, we got ourselves some unintended consequences. We're both smart people, but in that one respect we really screwed up. And we can be pretty certain that Uncle Jimmy is not a single individual acting on his own. We take him out, his brothers and his uncles and his cousins are going to try to connect the dots. We don't know what that would mean for Kira or for us. We know that probably none of it would be good."

I was having trouble meeting her eyes. I kept sitting within touching distance of her, but I had to bow my head a minute. "I just wish we could be sure we're not going to screw up again," I said. "Make things worse for Kira instead of better."

I made myself lift my head and face her directly again. My voice had gone whiny, and the sound of it was making me sick to my stomach.

Maura didn't look away, and her face conveyed a sadness like I had never seen from her before. I could see her thinking it through. I knew that all she really wanted when she got out of that car was to click the mouse on

Uncle Jimmy. She'd have vaporized him with napalm if she could have. So at least I'd pulled her back a little bit. But I doubted it made any difference. No question, Uncle Jimmy was long overdue for his trip to the land of was.

Maura closed her eyes, shook her head very slowly this way then that, opened her eyes again. This time she had no anger or impatience or even sadness in her expression. But oh Lord, her eyes were speaking to me, and I was pretty sure she was asking me, in spite of all I'd just said, *was I in or was I out?*

And all of a sudden I didn't know. Was this really what was wrong with me all along—that I wanted out? Had Uncle Jimmy and his pistol made me faint of heart? From weeks ago I'd been certain that I was in it with Maura all the way to the end, even if our destination turned out to be life in a cell without parole. But there I was, giving her pretty much the same slow head shake she'd just given me. This way then that, eyes closed.

But then we looked straight at each other, faces open, nothing that could be put into words—or even thoughts. But something. Something was definitely generating between the two of us, though I couldn't come up with the name for it—not desire, not affection, not exactly love, not unfinished business.

"I don't know, Maura." My voice was so weak I could barely hear it myself. I was just groveling—I felt disgusting.

She stood up. "You don't have to know, Jack," she said very softly. "I'll do it for you." She extended her arms to either side of herself. She tood waiting for me.

I wasn't sure why, but it took me half a minute to understand. But then I did, and I stood up opposite her.

I raised my arms until they were just like hers. Jesus and his twin.

She tilted her head.

"Oh," I said—and turned my back to her.

I felt her inch her body closer to my back. I felt her arms matched to mine behind me. Sardine Jesus. Jesus front to back. Weirdo double Jesus.

In a way I'd been trained for this. Not just by our having done quite a bit of moving together in the days just after Dr. Hatemo when we were getting used to each other. We hadn't done this in I didn't know how long. But we'd been through so much since then. In our fashion we'd lived hard. Now we were ingrown, like those old couples you see in restaurants who've been ordering the exact same dessert for about two hundred years and without saying a word to each other stand up from the table at the exact same instant.

We lowered our hands. We stepped sideways—her body still behind me, making me feel the count as if someone were chanting it aloud. Then, still body to body, we moved out through the door of the study to the living room. There we stood unmoving for maybe two full minutes. Breathing in unison. Maura's front touching most of my back, each of us inclining toward the other. I was lightheaded. Light-bodied, too.

Inhabiting Stillness, we would call this if we ever went professional.

Then it was as if we were floating back into memory. We step-slid to the photograph of Maura's mother. There we stopped to join her mother and inhabit her mother's stillness. We stood there until her mother nearly came back to life in my brain.

Then we slip-stepped and turned and stopped for our moments in the company of the cousins—Gertrude, Isabelle, Tasha, and Annie. Sweet girls, they greeted me like angels welcoming me in paradise.

And finally we moved a little away from each other, Maura signaling my body with her body to tilt and spin into giddy arabesques that finally placed us face to face with Grandpa Durham. The old coot with his chin jutting out like he dared us to take a swing at him.

It was while we were inhabiting Grandpa Durham's silence that the thought came to me. Grandpa Durham with his hatchet and his chickens was to Maura as my father with his pistol and his shot-up mirror was to me. I got a flash of living inside Maura's skin, looking over my shoulder, meeting the old coot's gaze with hers, steel for steel, fire for fire.

"Are you okay?" she asked. Her words were very soft, but she had nevertheless spoken them. "I thought I felt you shiver," she said.

⌘

We decided not to stop, not to sit down in the living room. We decided not to go to the bedroom, though I told her that was my truest desire. She nodded vigorously and said it was what she wanted, too, but it wasn't like the bedroom was going to detach itself from the house and we'd never see it again. "It'll be there when we finish," she said. "It'll be better then."

When we stepped back into her study, all the machines were waiting with their lights on and their little fans humming discreetly. They had nothing to say, of course, but if they had had words they would have been, *What took you so long?*

We sat down side by side and inhabited it until Maura had Uncle Jimmy identified and located. She sat back, sighed, glanced at me and blinked as if I had momentarily slipped her mind. She had no smile for me, but she rested her hand on my knee for just a second. Then she positioned the mouse on the desk exactly halfway between us.

We sat like that for a few moments. I was looking at the mouse; I was pretty sure she was, too. Maybe we were each waiting for the other.

She moved her hand on the desk until she could hold her finger directly over the mouse.

Then she tilted her head toward me. I moved my hand so it was beside hers, my finger also directly over the mouse. Our fingers were side by side. Touching.

"On the count of three," she murmured.

THE MEDITATIONS

Nothing I've ever done felt as rewarding as deliberately—
or "cold-bloodedly"—killing persons I wished to be dead.
Had I been forced into the presence of the person or had
I not felt completely immune from detection or pros-
ecution, I would have felt differently. Face-to-face killing
would have filled me with anxiety and fear. No matter how
clean and bloodless the method, I couldn't have done it,
couldn't even have come close. And actually witnessing
the death would have turned me catatonic. I use the word
"rewarding" deliberately, because "pleasure" was not my
experience. It registered with me like completing a difficult task that had been weighing on me for days. It felt
cathartic and energizing.

⌘

Those killings were initiated from a pleasant room that
served as a study for a professional person. Though I never
thought of doing so, I could have played music while I
committed the act. It was a room in a second-floor apartment in Georgetown, owned by my partner, Maura Nelson. Its two windows looked out into the branches of a
gingko tree, where cardinals, mockingbirds, sparrows, and

chickadees made stops on their way to and from their business. The room faced away from the street and was almost always quiet. It caught morning sunlight filtered by the gingko's limbs and leaves. There were Dufy prints on the wall and a maroon rug from Srinagar that covered most of the floor. I remember it as a place where I was often happy, though I'm aware of how perverse that sounds.

⌘

If I had her company now, Maura might shield me or distract me from what she would term my "ugly conclusions." Not that she deluded herself or attempted to delude me. It was just that she always mildly insisted on what she called "the context." "We don't transition these people in the abstract," she would say. "We choose individuals whose lives demand a radically ethical response." Well, I've never respected anyone as much as I did Maura, but I confess that I never bought into her idea of radical ethics. It just didn't work for me. She told me that what felt rewarding was eliminating the possibility of specific individuals to affect the world negatively. Not the killing. I hoped I'd come around to seeing it as she did.

⌘

If I deny the pleasure of killing, what do I do with the fact that I enjoyed it? When I sat back in my chair after clicking the mouse, I felt good. Doesn't it feel good to finally pay off one's mortgage, finish reading a difficult book, solve a challenging problem, complete a marathon that is utterly exhausting? I say that's not pleasure, it's another form of enjoyment. If Maura were listening to me make such an argument, she would smile indulgently. I do acknowledge that even as different as we were in our thinking, it was my personality and Maura's that made such killing so—I'll go ahead and say it—*appealing*. She would shudder at the sound of that word. And I would have to remind her that it was she who had once said, "I kind of hate us."

⌘

It's beyond me how Maura discerned that I'd be capable of having a discussion about killing people. I wouldn't have thought it either, and I certainly wouldn't have imagined describing how killing somebody could feel as rewarding as buying a house or sending a son or daughter off to college. My first words to Maura were, "Can you point me toward the periodicals room?" and hers to me were, "Why do you think I know where it is?" After she paused to size me up for a moment, she said, "Come on, I'll show you." My theory is that between her first spoken sentence to me and her second, something turned in the darkest chambers of her mind. She saw a capacity in me that I didn't know was there. And might never have known.

⌘

Normal people would probably argue that no matter how thoughtful a decision to murder is, actually doing it would not be *appealing* or *rewarding* for them. Anything but, they would say. But I suspect normal people would be hungry for more details. What about the guy who kidnapped the kid off a school bus and held him hostage in the bunker? Of that particular transition Maura and I enacted, a normal person might say, "Yes, I can see how that might have felt pretty good. To have taken that guy out, with no risk and no psychological damage to the boy—if you knew you could do that, maybe you wouldn't feel bad." They would try to come around to seeing it as Maura saw it—the correction of an obvious mistake in the traffic of human intercourse.

⌘

Some weeks after we had transitioned the bunker guy, Maura opened the door of her study and stood waiting for me to notice her. When I looked up from reading the *Times*, I realized it'd been a while since we'd talked. "Something to show you," she said, rather grimly I thought. So of course I followed her back into the study and took my seat beside her at the computer desk. The FBI had not only clandestinely inserted a microphone, they'd also managed to place a tiny camera eye into the guy's hidey-hole. Footage existed, though no government agency ever admitted as much. Citizens for Legitimate Government got wind of this, but was never able to find anyone who'd admit to having seen it. Encountering a stone wall from authorities at every level, CLG finally shut up about the matter.

Maura however, persisted. Sublimely talented hacker that she was, she used all her skill and knowledge to locate the footage and download it. "I want you to watch this with me," she said quietly and without checking my face to see if that was okay. The video had been edited from almost a hundred hours down to the final half hour of the life of Jimmy Lee Dykes. It began with a stretch of silence. The bunker interior was all shadows. A movement in the lower right corner suggested that the boy was sitting on the floor with a blanket around his shoulders. Dykes suddenly made a noise like a dog barking, stood up, and loomed close-up—his bearded face large and distorted. He uttered curses, as if he was speaking directly to the agents outside.

"Fuckers," said Dykes. "Sons of bitches," he squawked. He blocked our view of the boy. Then something distracted him. He turned away and walked toward the hostage. If he had a weapon, I didn't see it. He was gaunt and moved like his back pained him. "It's okay, honey," he crooned as if he was trying to sing. "They gonna send you in some Captain Crunch. And some milk, too. I asked them for milk." He stood up straight and stared upward, with his back still turned to the camera. His posture reminded me of those homeless veterans who haunt the sidewalk outside the Vietnam Memorial. Old men whose interior damage skews their bodies and faces. Standing over his hostage with his hands at his sides, the kidnapper was an instant away from my single click.

That was the exact moment I stopped wanting the man dead. Anyone who saw him then would recognize Dykes as a person whose life had brought him great harm. The noise we heard was his hostage sobbing. Suddenly Dykes's body jerked and contorted as if something inside him had exploded. His body lifted then fell. The hostage yelped just as his kidnapper hit the floor. We couldn't see him clearly. There was no sign he was moving. The only sound was that of the boy crying. Then three men in combat gear charged into the bunker and began firing their rifles downward—all three of them!—into the floor where Dykes had fallen. They fired many rounds. Maura switched off the video. We sat still, staring into each other's faces. "There you have it," she murmured.

Next morning we ate breakfast together. When we were both standing at the sink, as I was washing and she drying our dishes, she stopped what she was doing, turned, and said, "I know you don't believe me, but you should. What I know others will learn. And not very long from now. Untraceable killings will be as easy as making a phone call. It will happen like an epidemic. Hundreds every day. Then thousands. Millions. Nothing will stop it. Maybe the animals will find it amusing. We took the planet away from them. This will be how we give it back. We'll be so busy transitioning each other that we'll stop murdering the planet and everything that isn't like us." She nodded toward the window. Out there a white-throated sparrow sat on a tree limb, staring toward us. As if to say, "Fine by me."

⌘

I do question some things Maura told me, but I don't believe she meant to exaggerate how readily available her discovery was. She was just deluded the way a lot of smart but modest people are: *If I know it, anybody can know it.* She never spent much time around normal people. She had no basis for comparing herself to average citizens. She liked staying in her study with the door closed at least as well as she liked being with me. Even when our sex life was at its hottest, I had a sense that she could easily have turned away. When I review my years with her—as I do incessantly nowadays—I suspect that the thought of sex came to her only if I was around to remind her of the possibility. Not that I was anything special. On the contrary. For her it was an objective decision—*Oh, there he is—I can have sex with him. Yes, that's what I want.*

⌘

Why did Maura wait until she was thirty-nine to have sex with a man? And given that she'd waited that long, why did she choose me as the person who'd enable her to dispense with her virginity? We never discussed those questions in the time we had with each other. The first was the easier to address, and the answer I've settled on is conveniently simplistic: *It never occurred to her.* I believe that if an acceptable man had made an effort to seduce her, he very likely would have succeeded. At the very least, he would have brought the idea to her attention. As I did that first evening when she and I began making out on her sofa. When I think about those days now, our behavior seems to me as quaint as that of a nineteenth-century courting couple.

⌘

But why the life-changing turn in that instant between her two spoken sentences addressed to me in a library stairwell? It can't have been that she was swayed by my looks. It was a Saturday, I hadn't showered or shaved, and I doubt that I'd even tried to brush the bed-head out of my hair. After Vicki divorced me and before Maura and I took up with each other, I'd decided that my appearance made little difference to anyone, and so why bother keeping it up? I assume that what Maura saw was a man who would be no threat to her and one with whom she could converse without being bullied, manipulated, or provoked into argument. I doubt she felt even a sliver of sexual attraction to me—and so our becoming lovers must have seemed a collateral benefit that came with making me her confidante.

⌘

Peculiar as it may sound—though I would never say so in a courtroom—Maura and I were motivated by neither politics nor ideals. True, there was a pattern to our selections: They were mostly actively harmful right-wing zealots whose ambition had required them to abandon any semblance of integrity. In his mental illness, Jimmy Lee Dykes was an aberration, but Maura and I came to consider him as not so different from Justice Nino or Dr. Hatemo or most of the others we transitioned. It's just that Dykes's harm was focused on a semi-disabled five-year-old. Even the Junior Senator from Kentucky, whom we might very well have dispatched to his heavenly reward, was at least a cousin of Jimmy Lee Dykes, if not his brother in his thinking and fanaticism.

⌘

Both Maura and I considered ourselves thoughtful people, small-time intellectuals, but when it came to how we made our "selections," it was ninety-nine percent visceral passion: We wanted that person dead! Wanted it beyond rational thinking. Had we been religious people, we might have thought ourselves chosen by God to do His work, following in the path of Samson, Little David, or Joan of Arc. Which of course brings up the questions of exactly who we thought we were and what did we think we were doing? Good questions, because, really, without religion, ideals, or politics, we were acting without a history. We weren't aware of others who'd gone before us. There wasn't a path, there weren't any footprints. We were something new.

⌘

Maura and I occasionally fell into an ongoing conversation about John Richards, the very charismatic Democratic presidential candidate who fell into disgrace long before Maura and I met. We'd both been drawn to him, liked his message, believed in his integrity, then felt cruelly betrayed by the scandal he generated. "That he went to such extremes to cover it up demonstrates that you and I are gullible," I told Maura. "We'd have taken him out, wouldn't we? And there'd have been plenty of reason to do it, but we'd have done it mostly because he bamboozled us. Showed us that we weren't capable of making an accurate judgment. Showed us that we were just like every other American voter—foolish and confident in our choices."

"Chumps!" Maura said. "We wouldn't have liked it that he shoved it in our faces that we were chumps." But she was grinning. She liked it when we both got riled up and lectured each other like that. "At least John Richards was a liberal," I said. "And what he got busted for was pretty much what Kennedy got by with—*while he was in office*." "We both still love Kennedy, don't we?" she said.

168

"We're fools," I said. "So what are we doing?" she said. "I don't know," I said. "Talking about expediting somebody's trip to hell because he couldn't keep it in his pants," she said. She and I agreed we needed such discussions, even if they were like moot court or war games or acting-improv classes. Stimulating but not to be taken seriously.

John Richards showed us we needed an overflow moment. In Richards's case, the revelation of his chicanery was so gradual that he'd offered no single occasion that would have focused our loathing. "He'd have slimed his way past us," Maura said. That understanding set us back a bit. So we made ourselves an informal list of eligible candidates—persons we thought likely to need our services if they ever presented us with a new story, a quintessential TV interview, public statement, or televised performance. We agreed that our list shouldn't ever be written down. It had to be short enough that we could memorize it. I confess that our formulation of the list was recreational and a little silly. I doubt we realized that maybe we'd started down a dark path.

⌘

We liked reciting our list to each other or saying it aloud in unison. Horace Purvis. Bob O'Leary. John Arpaia. Ned Ruse. Ash Goodrich. Marcelle Halbgehirn. Mike Berry. Sylvester Alfero. The Cook Brothers (who counted as a single human unit, though we hadn't worked out how to transition the two of them simultaneously). Reverend Buddy Jones. Sally Pallid. Ronald Crump. Drew Dodds. Hank Shaughnessy. Rick Singer. Bill Scott. And after the shooting at Newtown—Dwayne LaPannier. We'd never heard of him but in a single day he soared to the top of our list. Most of the others had sufficiently outrageous personalities that we could enunciate their names with light irony. For Dwayne LaPannier I almost wished we had a maiming option.

⌘

Though we had decided that LaPannier might not need an overflow moment, he offered us one anyway. During the Senate hearings on the ban of assault weapons, national TV covered LaPannier's speech to the Texas Christian Coalition. His arrogance and his evil emerged in such plain view that he might as well have been dancing on the bodies of the dead children. To the families of those slaughtered first graders, each of whom had been shot several times, LaPannier had this to say: "The NRA's nearly five million members and America's hundred million gun owners will not back down—not now, not ever." When she heard those words splattering from his mouth, Maura stood up and aimed the remote at our TV and pressed the off button so hard it might have broken her finger.

She walked around the living room several times, sat back down, turned the TV on again but found the camera had tracked in for a close-up of LaPannier's smug face. The Texas Christians were applauding and roaring their approval while he beamed his approval over them. A little sheen of sweat showed on his forehead, his mouth was open in an ecstatic grimace that made it evident the man lived for moments like the one we were watching. He spread his arms out and opened his mouth wider to drink in the energy streaming to him from the audience, which brought forth a fresh surge from the crowd. Maura shut the TV off again and faced me as if to scorch me with her eyes. "It's him or me," she said. "I don't want to breathe oxygen he's breathed."

So we entered the study and did him. Maura had gotten better at keyboarding through the three stages, and while her fingers were busy, she made a confession. "That first time he spoke after Newtown? I looked up his DNA," she said. "I hope you don't mind. I wouldn't have done him on my own. I just wanted to be prepared." I told her it was fine, but I couldn't help wondering if she'd prepared the way for any of our other candidates. Or all of them? Wouldn't it make sense to get the necessary data on anybody who'd made our list? I wasn't troubled, because I trusted her. I just thought she was super-efficient. And had we considered it, we might have rushed from the study back to living room in time to see LaPannier drop behind the podium.

"Weak heart" was the conclusion leapt to by the entire nation. Right-wing crazies immediately cast LaPannier as an American hero, a man who had died while literally standing up for what he believed in. And death by natural causes worked perfectly well for the narrative they wanted. But if they'd known he'd been assassinated right before their eyes, that would have been even more effective for unifying the Republican Party. "We lost a great leader last night, but we found our purpose as conservative Americans," droned John Beamer. When Maura and I heard that clip, we were sitting at her kitchen table, listening to NPR news. We stared at each other, blinking.

"We actually made them stronger!" I said. "Why

didn't we anticipate that?" Maura asked. *Stupid* and *ignorant* were the words that occurred to me, but what I finally said was, "Because we didn't think it through?" She nodded.

It had seemed so simple, so obvious—and never more so than with the apotheosis of American idiocy, that sleek little monster who was the head of the NRA. Just delete the obscenity! Why wouldn't such an act instantly upgrade the world? While Maura and I sat at her table, I had this sense of our minds struggling against the evidence that what we'd done had had the opposite effect of what we'd intended. We'd helped the NRA! If for no other reason, we should go to prison for that. How long we sat there I couldn't say. Though it could have been my imagination, I felt our minds diverging. Against my will I began to question how solidly bonded Maura and I were. If we were so wrong in what we'd chosen to do, wasn't it likely that something was also wrong with what held us together?

⌘

Up until that moment love had not been the name of what I'd felt for Maura, but adoration might have been. Sometimes I'd fall into a trance just watching her hands nimbly managing a tea bag, a spoon, and a cup of hot water. What I felt for her wrists, her fingers, her arms, her lips, was akin to worship. But none of that emotion would have survived if it hadn't been for the extraordinary wholeness of her. The woman could absentmindedly put her hair up behind her head in a neat bun, she could move me around her living room in a strange dance, and she could silently

172

and invisibly assassinate a tyrant on the other side of the planet—and all of those aspects of Maura were as firm and whole as a fresh egg or a centuries-old Dutch painting.

Whatever the turns were that occurred in our interior lives in that moment at her table, they felt ominous to me. For the first time since our early weeks together, I became aware of the gap in our ages. Or I became aware of how what I thought to be the vast range, intensity, and delicacy of my feeling for Maura might have been a classic case of an old man's infatuation with a young woman. What I'd thought to be sublime might actually have been a cliché. However, there had been a moment when a hitherto unrevealed superwoman had stepped forth from the everyday Maura of my acquaintance. There in her kitchen, in my trance of recalling the day she sent Nino tumbling down the steps of the Supreme Court building, I felt both exhilarated and saddened. I realized that it foretold the end of us.

⌘

For what had seemed like eternity the word *Waste* had hovered in silence. Maura and I couldn't help hearing the faint noises that came from Kira's head in Uncle Jimmy's lap. Though he finally twitched and groaned and widened his eyes, he had never once stopped looking at us. I tried, but I couldn't tear my eyes away from him. Just when I decided I'd been frozen in the hell of having to stare forever at him with Kira's head resting on his thigh, he finally murmured softly to her, "Fix me back." Once again her hands rose to his pants on the other side of her head. Then my mind must have skipped a beat of time the way a needle on a turntable will skip a groove in a record. Maura had been sitting. Then she was standing.

Uncle Jimmy's hand had gone to the pistol on the table. Maura took a deep breath and stepped forward. "Shoot," she said. Uncle Jimmy lifted the pistol, then leveled his arm with it pointed at my belly. He wouldn't miss if he pulled the trigger. But Maura kept moving, and I wasn't afraid. "You don't want to hurt Jack," Maura said, almost flippantly, a teenager talking sense to a bully. "You've showed us what you wanted us to see," she said. "Message received." Kira looked up at her. Maura extended both hands to the girl to help her up. "I'm just going to put this child to bed," she told Uncle Jimmy. "Then we will say good night to you." Kira stood up. Maura put her arms around her. That's when I knew we'd get out of that room alive.

But what I also knew was that she would forever be the mensch, and I the helper, the assistant, the accomplice, the sidekick, the hanger-on, the gopher, the ignoble whatever. The imbalance wasn't news in any way other than that I realized I'd been fooling myself into thinking it might change. Or that I could change. Something would happen, and I would step up. Well, the pivotal event had just occurred, and I'd stayed sitting and speechless. After Maura and Kira slowly walked arm in arm down the hallway to the bedroom, Uncle Jimmy let his arm relax enough to be comfortable, but he kept the pistol loosely pointed in my direction. The smirk on his face told me what he was thinking. *Too bad you don't have the balls your girlfriend has.*

Maura stayed in the bedroom with Kira long enough that I began to think Uncle Jimmy might doze off. Finally she came into the room and gave me a nod. I stood up. He watched us and kept sitting with the pistol in his hand. If I'd been on my own I'd probably have stepped backward or at least sideways to the door. I would not have had the nerve to turn my back on him, but Maura gave him a nod—one that might even have appeared friendly—and turned deliberately toward the door. It was only when we'd stepped into the elevator and the door had closed behind us that she grabbed me with shocking force. While the elevator descended, she hadn't let go, and I'd felt her body gradually loosening. She must have been holding herself so taut for so long that now she was about to collapse. With my arm around her I'd half-carried her out of the hotel.

⌘

"It's like some science fiction creature that grows bigger, stronger and more vicious the more you shoot it or chop off its tentacles or throw grenades at it," Maura rasped out.

In her kitchen we were reckoning with our having given the NRA wackos new strength in their effort to put a gun in the hands of every man, woman, and child in America. Dead, Dwayne LaPannier was a hundred times more potent than he had been alive. With that between us, Maura and I stared at each other. I'd seen her furious and in deep sadness, but this was something else. "I don't know, Jack. I think we need to re-calculate. I thought we knew what we were doing." She put her face in her hands. "Are we just idiots?!" she moaned.

I knew where this was going, and something rose up in me that couldn't accept the idea that we were fools.

"This is just a setback." My voice surprised me with its confidence. "Look at Nino. He's gone, and we got somebody in there who's way better. Look at Jimmy Lee Dykes. He's out of his misery, and kids can ride school buses again without worrying they're going to be kidnapped by a freak with a gun." Maura gave me a sad look. "Dykes was about to be caught anyway," she murmured. "Why did we bother with him? We could have been a whole lot smarter there, too." Her voice was a barely audible mutter. "Maura," I said. I'd hoped I had words for her that would be convincing and powerful, but my brain didn't rise to the occasion. "Maura," I said again, and this time all I had to offer was, "I'm not ready to give up yet."

Once I said those words, an idea came to me. "You know this thing you stumbled upon? Your secret technique. That was like new science! It's not 'like,' it *is* a scientific discovery. And what we've been doing is testing it. Finding out what this science can do, how it ought to be used. Or ought not to be. In the long run even our mistakes are worth something. We're the techs in the lab wearing the white coats and writing on clipboards. This worked. This didn't. I agree with you that we should have realized that we're fallible. Our judgment is going to be flawed because we're human beings. But somebody needs to do what we've been doing. Can you think of anybody else you know that you'd want to be doing this?"

Maura kept giving me the fish eye, but I could tell she was processing what I'd said, not quite being able to disregard it. My idea that came from absolutely nowhere. I resisted the impulse to say more, but it wasn't easy to wait her out. "You understand that things have changed, don't you?" she said softly. Even if I didn't like the sound of her voice, I nodded. What choice did I have if I didn't want to give up on us? After a moment she sighed and turned toward the window.

I was pretty sure there was nothing out there she cared about seeing. She turned back to face me and sighed. "So you have a plan?" I could barely hear her. I wasn't ready for that particular question, but I trusted my mouth would provide me an answer if I just opened it. "I do," I said. "Hank Shaughnessy. The Cook Brothers. Rick Singer."

HOW WE LIVED IN THOSE MONTHS

"It's very dangerous if we start accepting lower and lower forms of behavior as the normal."

Maura was quoting Hank Shaughnessy, whom we had decided to send on his way. From the kitchen doorway where she stood drying the last of our breakfast dishes, she tilted her head in the direction of the study. She was signaling me that now it was time for the Fox News poster boy to go.

From the sofa I nodded, slipped off my shoes, and stood up immediately to take my place in front of the picture of Maura's mother. Maura and I had been quoting Shaughnessy to each other during the waiting period we had assigned ourselves. I had formulated some procedural rules, the first of which was that however distasteful it may be, we should acquaint ourselves with a candidate before we moved toward his transition.

Also, because I had come to understand that we both needed some relief from the grimness of our task, a few of my rules were whimsical. I had persuaded Maura that before one of us clicked the mouse we had to perform our dance in front of the pictures in her living room. The dance assignment replaced the sex that often preceded our moving into the assassination room. Maura agreed with me that our being aroused by the killing was profoundly wrong. We also agreed that the dance almost always pleasantly realigned us with ourselves and each other.

While I waited for Maura to join me at the place that was always our starting point I chattered at her. I was quite the blabbermouth in that phase of our relationship. "Here's something I want Jimmy Carter to tell a reporter," I said. "I want him to say, 'All I have to do to know that I have murder in my heart is watch Hank Shaughnessy's face on his show for maybe three minutes.'" This was the kind of remark I invented two or three times a day to help Maura keep her spirits up.

She snorted—which was as positive a response as I was likely to get from her on Shaughnessy. Last night she had told me she was sick of that guy before we ever began making our list. "Can't we just do him and move on?" she asked, and it was the first time I'd ever heard her sound whiny. I told her I thought we might be able to speed up the procedure. In his case there really wasn't much to discuss. Even the people who defended him did so on the grounds that the hard right needed a voice like his—loud, crude, and with complete disregard for the truth—to fight the socialist agenda of the left. Bill Moore said on his program last week that Roger Sales picked Shaughnessy for a reason: "The guy speaks for ignorant, racist, homophobic, and pissed-off America, and he does it from the heart."

"I define peace as the ability to defend yourself and blow your enemies into smithereens," I whispered to Maura when she took her place in front of me to face the picture of her mother.

"Smithereens is exactly what I'm looking for," Maura said, and the brightness of her voice encouraged me. She leaned back so that her shoulder blades were touching my chest.

"Nowhere in the Constitution is there this idea of the separation of church and state," I told her. While we arranged our hands and bodies together, I took up one of our favorite Shaughnessyisms, his making up a report from an Egyptian newspaper that the Egyptian government was considering a law that would allow a husband to have sex with his dead wife. "He's the living definition of the word *smarmy*. It's very difficult to find out anything about this man that doesn't argue strongly in favor of our granting him a visa to the Great Beyond," I intoned in my grand pronouncement voice.

Maura looked over her shoulder at me with her new look—the one that said, *I'm playing this game with you, because it's the only hope I have that we can make our way out of our hideous conundrum—that we can't go on and we can't stop—but don't believe for a minute that I don't see through you and your routines.* Then she nodded to signal our little slide to the left.

In this move across the floor, I became aware of what had changed about Maura's body. I could actually feel how much weight she had lost—and she had already been as thin as an addict. While we faced the pictures of her four cousins, who were forever eight, ten, eleven, and thirteen in my mind, I had this disturbing sense that their "Aunt Maura" had shrunk to the size of a child. My eyes teared up and blurred the faces of the cousins.

"Patrick and Merri Kelly," she told me quietly. "Shaughnessy has a boy and a girl." I knew she was saying those names because the sight of the photographs brought the mantra to her mind: *Gertrude. Isabelle. Tasha. Annie.*

Maura took a deep breath. "I know we're going to do him anyway, but let's not fool ourselves that there's no reason we shouldn't."

She had a point, but I didn't dare let her words hover between us without a response. "We'll be improving their lives by at least a hundred percent," I told her.

We took a long pause. Then she murmured, "Now the loop and twirl."

We moved apart and raised our arms to make the bridge. Maura slowly twirled away from me, twirled back again, so that now we stood side by side, each with an arm around the other's waist. "Now Grandpa Durham," she murmured.

The old man had been waiting with his sneer of contempt. And it wasn't Maura he was staring at, it was me! Somehow the old chicken-killer knew me better than I knew myself. Until I became Maura's partner in murder I had never completely come to life. I had wanted to live through my father, but he was too death-haunted to allow that. And my being thwarted by my father had made me unfit for Vicki in a way that neither of us could ever fix. Without Maura and her unusual capacity, I wasn't a man at all. If Grandpa Durham commanded me to chop a chicken's head off, I'd probably break into tears.

"Shaughnessy's a whore!" I made myself say. I wanted my voice to have the same jaunty intonation that Shaughnessy himself would use; instead, I was too loud, and my voice sounded shrill. Even so, I knew we were going to make our short pilgrimage into her study, where Maura was going to direct her fingers to tap the magic into her keyboard. Then she would slide the mouse over to me, and I would stare at it some moments during which time she would unabashedly observe my face. When I finally single-clicked Shaughnessy into oblivion, she would look away as if the sight of me immediately after a killing was just too repulsive to bear.

"Let's go give him the client of his dreams," I said. "The one he's been looking for ever since he flunked out of college."

"End of the dance?" she asked, glancing over her shoulder with a trace of a smile. She leaned her shoulders back against my chest and murmured, "It's very cozy here, don't you think?"

I knew what she was asking. Wouldn't I rather we went into the bedroom together? And had I not just received Grandpa Durham's condemnation of me, that would have been my choice.

"End of the dance," I said softly. Probably I was the only one who heard the sadness in my voice. But I was also the one who led the way through the living room and into her study.

PICTURE OF YOUTH

A picture of Maura and Ben and their parents appeared on the chest of drawers in the living room. That chest of drawers sat not directly beside the door to her study but near enough to invite a glance from anyone entering that room. The parents must have asked a neighbor to take the photo just before they got in the car to drive to church on Easter Sunday. Maura's mother and father and brother appeared to me to be the supporting cast for the daughter, who commanded the attention of the viewer—or at least that was the way this viewer interpreted the photograph.

Eleven years old and dressed up in a slim-fitting white blouse and knee-length pink skirt, Maura had brushed her hair until it shone, and her skin was pale as an apple blossom in the spring sunlight. *She looks nice* was the first thought that would occur to almost anybody. But the very quick next thought would be, *Man, that girl really doesn't want to go to church!* She was squinting, but it was her mouth that conveyed her high pout. If that shot were a video, you'd be certain the teenage girl was on the verge of turning her back to the camera, heading back into the house, and shouting over her shoulder, "I'm not going, I don't feel good!"

⌘

David Cook was one of the younger brothers. It was easier to hate him if you knew only a few things about him. He was the fourth wealthiest person in America. He had the standard right-wing view of the President as being a hardcore socialist who pretended to be somebody else. Cook's political views were those of a rich person who intended to keep on getting richer. He was against financial regulation, didn't believe in global warming, and generally opposed environmentalists. And he bankrolled the Tea Party. Because of the immensity of his wealth, he was a new kind of person on the political landscape—a billionaire activist. Which is to say that he tried to buy the kind of government he liked. One that let him do what he wanted.

But David Cook also opposed the war in Iraq, and he supported the arts, gay marriage, and stem-cell research. Not only that, he had played basketball for MIT and for many years had held the school's single-game scoring record of 42 points. I didn't know exactly why it was a redeeming factor in anybody's life to have been a fine athlete, but I wasn't immune to the concept. I did understand that to play basketball well you had to be an aggressive jerk, at least while you were on the court. There had been a few basketball players I had deplored—e.g., Bill Laimbeer, Ron Artest, Isiah Thomas when he walked off the floor and refused to shake hands with the Chicago Bulls who had just beaten his Detroit Pistons for the championship. But if I ever saw one of those guys in an airport, I would no doubt be thrilled and maybe even ask for an autograph.

I wouldn't ever see David Cook in an airport. Even if I do, an autograph won't be an issue. I wouldn't want it. He wouldn't give it.

⌘

I had been reading the *Times* on my tablet when Maura came out of the bedroom, heading toward the kitchen. She was in her pajamas. "I've never seen that photograph before, Maura," I told her. I grinned and nodded toward the chest of drawers by her study door. "Pretty nice picture," I said. We'd been deliberately sweet to each other since we'd dispatched Shaughnessy the previous week.

She shrugged, gave me a small, somewhat sleepy smile that could have meant she was feeling shy about the photo. She knew what I really wanted to know. *Why did you bring out that picture? What am I supposed to make of it?* "I just ran across it in my old papers," she said. "I couldn't stop looking at it." She paused a moment, glancing toward the window. "Or maybe I didn't want to stop looking at it." Her face suggested that this was a thought that had just arrived. "You don't mind that I put it there, do you?"

"No, not at all. I like it. But I don't think I've ever seen you in a pout like that. What were you mad about?"

Now she did smile. "I wasn't mad. I was just getting used to my braces, and they were really bothering me right then. I almost never wanted to go to church, but that morning I was fine with it, because my clothes were new, and all four of us were feeling pretty good. We'd had some very funny teasing going on while we were dressing up for Easter Sunday. Ben accidentally paid me a compliment. He said…He said, 'You look…'" Her smile still lingered, but then it just disappeared.

Her voice was a whisper. "That day was maybe a month or so before we found out about Ben's cancer."

We were both quiet, studying each other's faces. I was about to turn away, when she asked, "Maybe you have a picture you could bring out?"

I rolled my eyes because it had been so long since I even thought about a picture of me as a kid. At that moment it was like I hadn't even had a childhood. But that must have been what Maura had in mind—each of us making some kind of connection with our lives before we became adults. "I doubt it," I told her. "But I don't mind looking. Who knows what I might find?"

⌘

David Cook had three siblings, Frederick, Charles, and William. Through inheritance, all four had become billionaires, but David and Charles were the ones who used their money for political ends. Charles fancied himself enough of a philosopher to write a book called *The Science of Success*. Charles and David were the ones who had used their money to change the course of American politics.

Frederick had studied humanities at Harvard and received an MFA from the Yale School of Drama. Frederick collected manuscripts and gave his money to restore and protect historic properties. It was possible for people like Maura and me to think of Frederick as "the good brother." He and the youngest brother, Bill, had quarreled with the two older brothers, though they settled their differences through litigation.

It was Bill Cook who was evidently the spoiled brat of the four brothers—he was into yachting and collecting expensive objects like military vehicles. He was on his third wife, and he'd had some blow-ups with the previous wives that had gotten him arrested and made the news. If you just went by issues of character, then Bill was the one you'd give a priority rating as a candidate for transitioning. Trouble was, he was just your basic spoiled rotten piece of oil-rich trash. Hardly worth the effort.

⌘

To look for a photograph of myself as a kid I had to drive back to my old apartment. Though I had continued paying the rent on the place, I'd gone for weeks without thinking about it, and I hadn't actually stepped inside for several months. In its dim light I felt like I'd been living in an exotic foreign country but now I was returning home where nothing exciting ever happened. I opened shades, turned on lights. I walked slowly into my old office and sat down at the desk, which I had left in a perfectly tidy state when I went to live with Maura. The neatness of the desk told me that I'd been pretty certain I was never coming back.

I was struck with the idea that my old life as a person of no consequence had been waiting for me to pick it up again. Silly idea, but I could just stay there. Call Maura and tell her I wasn't coming back. The instant I imagined our conversation—"You're what?" she would ask.... I'm certain it wasn't what I wanted to do, but that line of thinking wouldn't stop teasing me. No more conundrum. No more struggling to keep Maura's spirits up and to prevent our relationship from unraveling.

Sitting at my old desk I fell into a bit of a trance. Where I was besieged by random visions. Patrick and Merri Kelly Shaughnessy sadly going back to school after the month of grieving over their dad's death. Dr. Hatemo's mansion still being tended by his household staff as if the old son of a bitch were still alive and well. Jimmy Lee Dykes as a boy sitting at a card table assembling model airplanes with his dad on a Saturday afternoon. David Cook clambering out of the crash of US Air Flight 1493 on the runway of the Los Angeles Airport. It was that latter image—or mental video—that really unsettled me. Thirty-six people had died in that crash, but Cook was among the ones who came out of it alive. He was also a cancer survivor, he was seventy-three years old, and now I wanted to take the years he had left away from him? What kind of idiocy was I up to? I mean, if I wanted to kill an old man, let it be Dick Clancy, who had never shown the slightest bit of remorse or doubt about his evil acts.

But in that chair in my old familiar room—where my only questionable behavior had been to earn money through some educated guessing—I suddenly experienced a powerful temptation to leave my life with Maura behind me. To just stay here in this steady peace and quiet. To be a person of no consequence again—by choice. I found myself taking the thought seriously. What are we other than the amalgamation of our fears and our desires? I felt shaken by forces that were far beyond my understanding. I sat with my thoughts a while, the way I sometimes did when I was trying to evaluate a company whose stock I was considering buying. As a day trader I had no special skill, but I did have common sense. And I had the patience to sit quietly and think hard about a decision that might make or lose several thousand dollars.

Funny thing was, the room itself—and the serenity it offered me—made its own case. Sure, I hadn't even thought about buying or selling for some months, but I could have this space. And it was extremely soothing. And yet the longer I sat still in that room—and if I wanted I could sit there all day—the more urgently I wanted to be back in Maura's presence. Or at least her proximity. I made myself sit tight and think hard. But I wasn't really thinking. I was trying to see my life with Maura from there on out—painful, crazy, most likely heartbreaking—and comparing it with what would happen if I stayed there. Extraordinary days as opposed to endless hours of almost nothing whatsoever.

⌘

In my folder of old photographs, there was one of toddler me with golden curls and a sweet smile. Another one presented college boy me with my two brothers posed in front of the forsythia bush of our parents' backyard, all three of us in jackets and ties—we looked like frat boys. Yet another revealed high school me flirting with my first girlfriend beside the punch bowl at somebody's birthday party. The one I chose, however, was a formal portrait I'd inscribed for Grandma Lawson when I was in eighth grade. I was in my band uniform, standing very straight and holding my plumed hat beside my right hip. I wore a braid on the opposite shoulder and triangles of braid descended along that left sleeve. My grin had a slight curl of teenage scorn, but mostly what was evident was my pride. It was obvious that I thought I looked terrific in that foppish, semi-military costume. My white buck shoes were immaculate, and I'd had a recent haircut—a flattop as it was called in those days.

I was fourteen years old in that picture. Something

else that was present—and this must be the reason for my picking it—took me several minutes to discern. Along with the obvious vanity, my face could not have been any more open in its display of softness of character. I was accustomed to being loved by my family. I was willing to do just about anything in order to be liked by my friends and acquaintances. I secretly, desperately, urgently wished to be admired by everyone. The statement that photograph would make to Maura was that as a boy Jack was malleable. Jack didn't really have a palpable self. Jack could be molded to suit another person's needs.

I got a little shock when I realized that Maura almost certainly already knew this about me. She'd have been surprised that I didn't know it about myself.

On the way back to Maura's place I stopped at a Dollar Store to buy a cheap frame. When I stepped into her apartment, the bedroom door was closed—she must have been napping—and so I had the living room to myself. I arranged the photograph of fourteen-year-old Jack to sit parallel to the one of eleven-year-old Maura. When I stood back to get some perspective, I couldn't stop looking. My mind worked at seeing those two children in the same world. I could almost imagine them meeting and trying to hold a conversation. "Hey," one of them would say, and the other would reply, "Hello," and then they'd have trouble going on from there.

⌘

I picked up my tablet and sat down on the sofa where I had a view of the photographs on the chest of drawers. I was in a haze of thinking about those kids—and how they couldn't have dreamed of what would become of them in their grown-up lives. I expected Maura would soon wake up from her nap and open the bedroom door. But she surprised me by coming up the stairs from the street entrance, unlocking the front door, and entering. Her face was flushed. When I raised my eyebrows, she shook her head and grinned. "I think I'm ready for the Cook brothers," she announced. She had something to tell me, but she was saving it. Her voice was bright, her face animated. She could have been about to tell me she had discovered an easy way we could save ourselves from what we'd become. It was how she spoke of the Cook brothers that put me off. We'd never been casual, never treated anyone—even Shaughnessy—like a pesky little task we had to take care of.

"I'm not sure," I said. "They're too complicated for me. The one I could send on his way with not much ambivalence is Bill Cook, but that's just because he's useless and trashy."

Maura's happy face turned serious. She took off her sweater and sat down beside me—close enough that I felt the excitement her body was still generating. That seemed odd to me, and I thought I might have to remind her about our new rules. Didn't we usually sit across from each other when we were discussing a candidate? But then the coziness of her sitting beside me had a tonic effect. "What's up, Maura," I asked softly.

"Oh," she said, standing up again. She had just noticed the picture of me in my band uniform. She walked over, picked it up, and stood there to study it. Because her back was to me I noticed the very slight movement of her head as her eyes moved from my photo in her hands to hers on the chest of drawers. "This is good," she said, turning to catch my eye. "This is a way I'd never thought of you," she says. "Sweet boy looking very militaristic."

When she returned the photograph to the chest of drawers and walked back to the sofa, her smile was one I couldn't resist. I considered suggesting we go into the bedroom where we could be comfortable. I didn't say anything, though—she was back beside me, near enough that our hips and shoulders were touching. "I think those two kids are just what we needed, don't you?" she asked.

I had to think a moment. "Some couples make babies to save their marriages," I said. "This could be like that, I guess."

"Like we've given birth to ourselves?" she said with a chuckle.

"Maybe they're talking me out of doing the Cook brothers," I told her. "I'd been trying to make myself believe it would be a good thing to take those guys out of politics. To stop that river of cash from flowing into the Tea Party's bank account. But I keep seeing them in these family settings. Four boys trying to stay on good behavior while they eat dinner with their parents in the formal dining room. Or playing croquet on Sunday afternoons on the great lawn of the mansion in Wichita. Four rich boys—it must have been a pretty rowdy childhood they had."

Maura studied me. Her face was pleasant, friendly, interested. "Have we ever changed our minds?" she asked. "Decided not to do somebody?"

"Well, we didn't get around to the Junior Senator from Kentucky that time," I reminded her. "He was on our radar, but then we got distracted. It's too bad. Every time

I see that guy's picture I think we should have bought him a ticket. He's definitely going to run for President. He'll give the loonies a loony to vote for."

We just sat quietly, and it felt okay to me. Like something was turning for us, turning in our favor.

"No Cooks, huh?" Maura said.

"You don't sound that disappointed," I said.

"They've always seemed far away," she said in a dreamy voice.

I stayed quiet. She was thinking out loud, and I wanted to see where she was going.

"They don't make the papers, we don't see them on TV," she said. She was relaxing into the sofa, and so was I. "Which probably means they're doing more harm than the people we do read about and see all the time," she murmured.

"Like Rick Singer?" I asked. I kept my voice low, maybe just because we were sitting so close beside each other.

She shifted a little and leaned forward to look me in the face. "You don't think we're going to talk ourselves out of doing him, do you?"

"God, I hope not," I said. The minute I said the words, I got a scary thought. Maybe it didn't really matter who it was or how much they deserved to be sent on their way. Maura and I just needed to do somebody.

Anybody.

A silence came down on us, which made me think Maura had had the same thought I had. What was even scarier was that I wasn't put off by it. Not horrified at all.

"Want to do Rick Singer right now?" I whispered.

Our silence hung in the air a long moment.

"Just stand up and walk in there and do him? You and me? Right this second?" she whispered. "What about our rules?"

I shook my head. Our eyes were beaming into each other's faces. The air felt electric.

I stood up. Maura was only a split second behind me.

⌘

Any thoughtful person would wonder if we ever killed someone accidentally. Here's the unfortunate truth. We thought we did. We didn't know for sure, but we were pretty sure we did. Natalie Harmon. Mother of two, thirty-five years old. A brilliant, articulate Lutheran pastor, who had just moved from Manhattan to Arlington, Texas. "These people need a responsible voice for the gospel a lot more than the folks who attend Riverside," Pastor Harmon had said about her new congregation in a radio interview.

Maura and I thought we made Natalie Harmon dead with an error that occurred in Maura's first try at deleting Dwayne LaPannier. She had accidentally pressed Enter before she'd fine-tuned her calculations. It was the kind of error computer users make several times a day. The good lady pastor turned up with a stopped heart the same day as LaPannier did. She had been in excellent health, and there was no plausible explanation for her death, except for the one that only Maura and I grasped in the instant we read about it in a little Internet news posting. Pastor Harmon and LaPannier died about a block and a half away from each other, and there was only about a ten-minute time difference between her death and his. Computer error, or coincidence? Especially worrying was the possibility that Maura's calculations were slightly off or that I had distracted her at a crucial moment.

When we read about Natalie Harmon, Maura and I understood something awful about ourselves—that we couldn't make ourselves feel anything about having killed the woman. Maura even looked up her obituary in *The Miami Herald* online and read it aloud to me. I listened all the way to the end. Then we sat quietly, waiting, I think, to take hold of the horrific despair that refused to come to us and that seemed just out of our reach. We were sitting across from each other at Maura's kitchen table. I knew I should, but I couldn't feel anything much beyond my righteous certainty that even if it had energized the NRA we'd done the right thing in ridding the world of that atrocity Dwayne LaPannier. "Collateral casualty," I finally said, keeping my voice as low as I could. Maura nodded and tightened her lips. "Thank you for the language," she said. "Natalie Harmon was a collateral casualty. It helps to have the words for what ought to make us feel terrible but doesn't."

⌘

It took maybe five minutes from when we entered Maura's study to Maura sliding the mouse over to me and my single-clicking Rick Singer to send him on his way. Then we leaned back in our chairs and studied each other. We hadn't turned on any lights because the afternoon sun was shining through the window. But now that light was softening. The change was just what we needed. The moment was perversely revealing, because I thought we had demonstrated to each other that we were equally hooked on clicking somebody into oblivion. But it was also weirdly sweet because our damaged connection had healed itself. We had come back together, and it felt very, very right. "Maybe we should send Rick Singer a thank-you note," I said, clasping my hands behind my head and leaning back in the chair.

"Where would we send it?" Maura asked.

"Thirteenth circle of Hell," I said.

Maura laughed very softly. Then she said, "Jack?"

"Yes, Maura," I said.

"I have to tell you something."

"Oh Lord," I said.

I sat up straight in the chair and looked directly at her. She sat up, but she couldn't seem to make her eyes meet mine.

"I've been in touch with Kira," she said.

I was expecting much worse news, but I didn't say so. And I didn't really know what that news would have been, maybe that Maura wanted me to move out of her place. I knew it was smug of me, but I couldn't imagine her taking up with somebody else, man or woman. She might very well have thrown me out, but it would have been because she wanted her solitude back. Or because she wanted to break her transitioning habit.

"And?" I finally said.

"And I told her maybe she could come live with us. I told her I'd talk to you about it."

REUNION

"Who got in touch with whom?"

"I did. I'm sorry I didn't let you know I was looking for her. I thought there was a good chance I wouldn't be able to find her. Then when I found her, I wasn't sure what I'd do. Also I knew you'd disapprove. Even if you didn't say so."

I shook my head. I didn't want to argue, especially since she was probably right. "Why did you look for her?"

Maura took a minute or so of staring at her lap before she answered that question. Finally she said, "I've always had this fantasy of rescuing somebody."

"So you made contact with her."

"Yes."

"How did you do that?"

"You know me and locating people. She's here in DC, but I couldn't get a fix on where she was living. Evenings and mornings she'd show up in one location, then another, but she went to the National Gallery just about every day. And she stayed long hours, so I knew she must have been working there. I even went there a couple of days to see if I could catch sight of her, but no luck. It was like she was there, but she'd figured out a way to be invisible."

"And?"

"And I kept thinking if she was in DC, there was a good chance she knew we lived here, and eventually she'd make contact. So I waited, even though it made me feel crazy. I'd found her, but I couldn't see her."

"Did she come to DC to find us?" This concerned me. I didn't want to open my front door one morning and find Uncle Jimmy's twin brother waiting for me.

"Not exactly. She thought we might be here, but she didn't know for sure. And she didn't plan to get in touch with us. She just thought it might be a happy coincidence if she ran into us somewhere in town."

"So how did you make contact?"

"One day I had lunch in that restaurant that's on the first floor of the museum. I watched the wait staff going in and out of the kitchen. When the doors opened I heard the voices of the cooks. The light bulb in my brain lit up. She was working in that kitchen. I'd probably never get to see her unless I walked in there and looked around. Or saw her going in or out."

"You were right?"

"Took me a couple of afternoons of waiting outside the service entrance. And even then I had trouble picking her out. She wore sunglasses and a hat. Also disgusting jeans. She's a dishwasher. Her hair's really short now, almost a buzz cut. It's like she's decided to look the opposite of the way anybody who knew her before would expect her to look."

"But she was glad to see you?"

"I got a hug that nearly broke my ribs."

"So what's her story?"

"She knows her 'relatives' are looking for her. She

thinks it's just a matter of time before they find her. She says she's worn out from being on the run. She says it will be very bad for her when they find her. They will make an example of her. She says they will want it to be in the news, and they will make it so grotesque that every one of their girls will get the message."

"Okay."

"You think it's crazy I mentioned to her that maybe she could live with us."

Maura would have known it in an instant if I tried to lie. I shrugged.

"I have a plan," she murmured. "I hope it won't upset you," she said.

I nodded. She knew there was not a lot she could do that would upset me. "I'd expect no less of you," I said. Then I asked, "Does your plan include where she's going to stay when she lives with us?"

"This might upset you," she said. But she didn't look away when I caught her eye. She sighed and stood up. Tilted her head to signal that I should follow her.

We walked into her bedroom and to her dresser, where from the top drawer she extracted a small key ring with a couple of keys. Then she led me back out to the living room to the door beside the closet where we hung our coats. A door that I'd never seen unlocked. A door that she told me led to a utility room. She'd never mentioned that she had the keys. Now she opened that door and stepped through it and switched on a light. I followed her, and we stood just inside the door. There was a stack of boxes in there and another stack of what looked to be computer modules. But there was also a sofa and a chair and a TV and even a tiny little kitchen.

I gave her a look. Eyebrows raised.

She shrugged. "I pay the rent on it," she said. "I needed the storage space, and I thought it might come in handy sometime."

We were standing in a room that was completely strange to me but one that had been there all along. And Maura did a strange thing, or what would have been a normal thing but which she'd never done in all the time I'd been with her. She lifted her hand and touched my cheek in a kind of caress. I'd have sworn the look on her face was one of pleading. And I'd never before seen her look like this.

"You're wondering what other surprises I might have for you," she said. "I don't blame you. I'd feel the same way if I were you."

I waited to see if she'd say more. When she didn't, I raised my hand and set it ever so lightly on her hair. I had wanted to do that ever since I'd met her, but only now that she'd touched me had I felt I could touch her like that. But I got the sense that she couldn't bear it for very long. So I took my hand away quickly.

⌘

It was some minutes before Kira could bring herself to look directly at me, which I took as an invitation to scrutinize her. From what Maura had told me, I'd expected her to have a rough appearance. She was bone thin, yes, but what shocked and amused me was that she stank—and not just the odor of a body that hadn't been washed for some days. The girl carried with her into Maura's apartment the stench of rotting vegetables, of kitchen garbage.

Also her demeanor was servile, suspicious, fearful. She seemed to be trying to minimize her presence, trying not to call attention to herself. I was surprised I hadn't noticed that earlier when she was under the abusive control of Uncle Jimmy. But of course it must have been living on the street that had diminished her so much. Maura and I had seen how Uncle Jimmy cultivated her potential for looking elegant, whereas being on her own in DC had turned her into a human rat.

When Maura first escorted Kira into the apartment, the two of them had been shopping, and Maura had bought Kira new underwear and slacks and tops and shoes. Before dinner that evening, she showed the girl into the bathroom of the little apartment and stayed in there with her while Kira showered and changed into clean clothes. Maura carried out the girl's filthy jeans and t-shirts in one of the shopping bags that had carried in the new ones. "This is all she has to her name," Maura said as she passed by me on her way out to the back entrance and the dumpster. I grinned at how she had taken on a motherly role. Before my eyes, she'd become cheerful, wholesome, and practical in a way I would never have anticipated.

At dinner that evening, Maura gently told the girl that she had to stop working at the museum if she wanted to stay with us. "Your relatives will see that when you leave work you always come here. They will knock on our door. I'm sure you know that," she said.

Kira was evidently hungry and enjoying the pasta I'd fixed for us—she didn't stop eating to answer. "Yeah, sure," she said, lifting her fork for emphasis. "No problem." Then she shrugged and looked from one to the other of us and said, "Just tell me what you want me to do."

We smiled at her—Maura and I were both touched by how hungry she was and how vulnerable she appeared to us. But neither of us knew what to tell her. It was a question that lingered with Maura and me on into bedtime.

"What exactly do we want her to do?" I asked Maura when she came into our bedroom after saying goodnight to Kira. I set aside my book while she changed into her nightgown.

"I suppose she thinks it's sex," Maura said. "And she's probably just waiting for us to find a delicate way to convey that to her. And here's what's scary—I think she'd be fine with that."

I smiled at her. "Well, I can't speak for you," I said.

Maura shook her head as she slipped under the covers. "You and I are complicated enough. And it would be wrong in at least half a dozen ways. Freaks me out even to imagine it."

"So that brings us back to the question."

"Yes, it does. But I expect you know the answer. Or if you think about it for a while, you'll know it."

I was pretty sure I did know the answer, but it was troublesome, and I wasn't eager to say it aloud. We were both quiet a moment or two while we settled in beside each other.

"How much information do you think she has?" I finally asked.

"You mean names? Places? She has a lot, I'm pretty certain. But there must also be plenty she doesn't know. And in this case, these people are so far away from my area of expertise that our margin of error will be huge."

"But the people who are working here in the States—I expect she knows who most of them are, don't you?"

"Yes, that's right. Even so, lots of room for mistakes."

I let some time pass. Disturbing though this conversation was, it nevertheless felt cozy to be there in bed beside Maura. We were not up to anything, we were just talking. "This is my comfort zone," I said.

"Mine, too," she said. And by her tone of voice, I was sure all over again that I would follow this woman into hell.

"So we know we're going to do this, don't we? By 'this,' I mean the new direction we're going to take, the words we don't want to say aloud."

Maura didn't answer right away, but I suspected it was more because she was enjoying the hiatus. We were not going to continue as we had, but we were about to take up something that was equally problematic. Now we were more deeply and permanently connected than we had been. The world out there might be more threatening than ever, but in our solidarity she and I were ready to face it.

"Yes, we know it," she said finally.

I, too, waited a moment before moving the conversation along, "Are we in a hurry?"

"The longer we wait to get started the more likely it is that they'll show up looking for her."

I felt the rising concern in Maura's voice. Even just talking that way, we'd started moving toward danger. But we both understood that we were not likely to turn back.

"So that brings up the next question. Should we trust her?"

Maura actually sat up in bed to answer me. "Well, we can't, really," she said, "because she's been so damaged. Poor kid," she said.

"But we have to proceed as if we trust her, don't we?"

I said. "Because we can't proceed at all unless we let her know more about us than is safe."

Maura studied me a long moment. "Okay, Jack. We do know what we're talking about here, don't we? *Safe* isn't any good to us any more. We need to take this risk."

Now I studied her for a couple beats. "So we trust her. Or pretend to ourselves that we trust her. Even though we're very likely going to pay for it."

Maura nodded gravely. "We should try to get used to her before we have that conversation with her," she said.

"So we have some time," I said.

"Not much, but a little," she said. "A few days maybe."

Then she turned out the light on her side of the bed, I turned out the one on my side, and we moved against each other's bodies, nestled up and spooned like an old, long-married couple.

⌘

The new quality about Kira that I suddenly understood the next morning was a kind of neutrality of identity. She'd gone generic, nearly sexless, non-specific.

Also surprising to me was how Kira's appearance here had enabled me to think of this space as *our* living room—Maura's and mine. Until then I'd thought of all that space as belonging to Maura. It was odd—evidently if Kira was here, then I could think of the apartment as half mine. If Kira were not here, then it would go back to being Maura's. Either way, I didn't think of it—even the tiny little apartment—as belonging to Kira. I thought of her as something between a guest and an intruder. And even after she could manage to look directly at me, it was just a glance. She didn't want to meet my eyes, didn't want to engage in conversation with me alone.

⌘

By our third day together, Maura and Kira and I had entered a phase of living as a peculiar family. That was how it would be if Maura and I had adopted the girl. We had our meals together—and that evening when Kira volunteered to fix dinner, she managed a tuna salad, the old-fashioned way that used canned tuna, with lettuce and tomatoes. Kira was inclined to shadow Maura, following her from the living room to the kitchen and back, though she tried to be unobtrusive about it. And she found excuses for inviting Maura into her own living space. I got used to hearing the murmur of their voices behind that now-unlocked door. I did get a little paranoid over Kira's avoiding situations that would place just the two of us in a room together for an extended period of time. And over the fact that she almost never asked me any questions, whereas she seemed to have a hundred things to ask Maura. But I understood that the first lesson of her life must have been that she was likely to be better off if she kept her distance from men. All in all, the three of us became accustomed to the necessary adjustments we had to make for each other.

⌘

On the fourth day of our ménage a trois, at the moment when we would ordinarily have stood up to begin clearing the table of our dinner dishes, Maura caught my eye then turned directly to the girl. "Kira, Jack and I think we might be able to help you. We have something we'd like to discuss with you."

Kira blinked, sat up straight, flicked her eyes in my direction, then faced Maura. I could have sworn I saw her taking a deep breath. She must have been thinking, *This is it—they're going to tell me what they want from me.* She gave me another quick glance as if to try to estimate how awful it would be to have to commit sexual acts with me.

Maura sat back in her chair, giving the appearance of being relaxed, though I was certain she was worried about how this conversation would go. Her voice, however, was steady and businesslike. "We may be able to solve the problem of your relatives who are trying to find you and make an example of you."

Kira nodded very slightly. She, too, must have been deeply anxious.

"Jack and I have a way...We can...."

I sympathized with Maura's struggle to find the right language to explain to the girl exactly what it was that we had to offer her. Even between the two of us, we often couldn't bring ourselves to say what we meant. She gave me a quick grimace, then took a deep breath, looked back at Kira, and made herself say it.

"Kira, Jack and I have discovered how to kill people if we think there's a good reason for them to die." Maura's voice sounded as flat and expressionless as if her vocal cords had been replaced with a mechanical device in her throat. She paused. Both of us were so focused on Kira's face that our eyes might have been generating heat.

"We can do this without being detected. We can kill them and leave no trace."

There it was. What we could do. And even in my mind, I was aware of how correct she was to use the term "we." She was the one who knew the secret, but I had become the one who activated the power. *We* did it. *We* killed without being detected. Evidently I didn't think of it as I used to—I felt something like pride when I heard Maura say those words aloud.

The apartment was so quiet I could imagine I heard the little clicks of Kira's eyelids touching when she blinked. The stillness lasted too long. Then Kira's hand slowly lifted beside her face and the fingers of that hand opened.

"Anybody?" she whispered, leaning forward. "You can kill anybody?"

Maura nodded.

Kira looked at me and didn't look away.

I nodded, too.

"My relatives?" she whispered.

Maura and I nodded.

Kira closed her eyes and kept them closed. "What do you need from me?" she whispered.

"Their names," I said. "And where they are. To the best of your knowledge. And any information you can give us to help us identify them—to be sure that we don't mistake them for someone else."

"And we need to know the ones you think are looking for you now. The ones who'd be likely to find you first."

Kira nodded but kept her eyes closed and said nothing.

After a moment, Maura said very softly—as if her human voice had been returned to her—"Can you do that, Kira? Can you give us their names and the information about them that we need?"

Kira's eyes snapped open, and now they were the ones

that seem to be generating heat. "Fucking-A I can do it! Do you know the poet Akhmatova?" She looked from one to the other of us.

I nodded. Maura shook her head.

"I am like Akhmatova," Kira said. Her voice was strong, and evidently it made no difference whether or not Maura and I knew anything about the great Russian poet. "I remember every awful thing," she said. "And every name. Every man's face and who he is and who his father was. I can give you everything and even more than that."

❋

The first telling session started immediately. Maura sat down at the table to take notes while Kira and I cleared the table and put the kitchen in order. Kira was only a little help, because she kept moving and talked the whole while. But of course that was exactly what we wanted her to do. Her face became flushed and animated as she spoke. This was a new Kira altogether. She could hardly finish speaking about one man until she had to take up another. Not only was she astonishing in the amount of detail about these men she had stored in her mind, she was also freakishly aware of which men were pursuing her now, where they were likely to be at that moment, and how long it would take them to find her. "If you can't stop them, Yury and Pyotr will walk through that door...." She pointed to Maura's front door as if those men were already standing out there in the hallway. With a fearful look on her face she nodded toward that door. "Tomorrow afternoon. Or the next morning."

"They're that close, Kira?" I asked. I was stunned by

208

this information. And suddenly fearful myself. Somehow I had started believing that Maura and I were untouchable.

"Those two," Kira said, shaking her head. "Those two enjoy the cat and mouse. And they make the one you call Uncle Jimmy look like your American Easter Bunny."

Maura and I just stared at the girl. She stared back at us, blinking and shaking her head, as if we couldn't possibly know such people as Yury and Pyotr. "I would have had to leave here tonight. Or else be ready to go with them tomorrow when they come."

⌘

A little after midnight Maura set aside her pen, shook her aching hand, and with a little grimace made an announcement. "We have viable candidates for the foreseeable future," she told us. Kira had provided us with the names of fifteen men and what Maura thought was sufficient information about them for us to send them to their hellish reward. Kira said she had knowledge of another fifteen to twenty men and women who should also be considered candidates. But at that moment, we needed to take urgent action only on the two who had been closing in on her in recent weeks—Yury Chirkov and Pyotr Maletski.

"I assure you that tonight they are sleeping in the Willard Hotel," Kira told us, her face twisted with her distaste for imagining Yury and Pyotr in their luxurious quarters. "I don't think you want to know how I have such knowledge of them, but I will tell you that too, if you think it necessary."

Maura and I exchanged looks, then we shook our heads at Kira. To each other we were acknowledging that we were deep in our pretend-trust of the girl. For all we knew Kira could be working for the organization that we'd been given to believe was intent on kidnapping and/or murdering her. But at that point we had no choice about how to proceed. I was a little surprised at how cheerful Maura seemed to feel about the situation. Then I realized that I, too, felt irrationally comfortable with what we were about to do. We were both probably feeling some lift from Kira's energy and conviction.

With Kira suddenly having nothing more to tell us and the dishwasher having finished its cycle, the whole apartment felt extremely quiet. For some minutes the three of us continued sitting at the kitchen table. Kira monitored our faces. Maura and I beamed reassuring smiles toward her and toward each other. The thought occurred to me that sometime in the future I was likely to recall those minutes as the moment when the three of us became co-conspirators.

"All right," Maura said, standing up and gathering her notes. "Look out, Yury. Look out, Pyotr. Enjoy your dreams now, because we're coming to get you."

I stood up, too, and I nodded at her to acknowledge the exuberance of her phrasing. Kira stayed sitting but her face indicated she wanted us to tell her what to do. I knew that Maura and I firmly believed she would go into the room with us, but we hadn't given her even a clue about what we would do once we were in there.

Then Maura gave me as peculiar a look as I'd ever seen on her face. She stepped over beside me near enough that our arms were touching. "Jack," she said very softly, "do this with me. I want Kira to watch us."

My expression must have been conveying to her that

I had no idea what she meant. "Don't worry," she said, turning her back but stepping directly in front of me, then leaning back so that her shoulder blades touched my chest. "We'll be fine. She will understand."

Then I knew what she had in mind, and though I recognized how wildly odd her idea was, I felt exhilarated. Maura was the one person who in that circumstance would take action. And I was the one person who could appreciate her plan and collaborate with her. I slipped off my shoes and put my arms lightly around her, my fingertips to her elbows.

"First to Kira," she said. "Two steps forward." From her back against my chest I felt exactly when to take the steps. Once there, Maura took my left hand in hers, stepped away from me to make a little curtsy to Kira—and I knew to bow slightly until Maura stood up straight. Then she took her place back in front of me.

"Sideways to visit you know who," she said softly, and we slid that way, as nicely in unison as if we'd rehearsed the steps. And indeed we had, though it had been some weeks since we'd done our mystery dance. I was absurdly happy to do those steps with Maura. The ritual itself had always pleased me, but to do it there with Kira as our audience lifted me a notch or two higher.

For Kira's benefit Maura said, "My mother." She and I stood before the picture as if waiting for that lady's blessing. Once again Maura's mother's expression, with those widened eyes, took hold of me, but this time it felt as though she was in cahoots with both of us rather than with just long-ago Maura in the act of photographing her.

"Now to my cousins," Maura murmured. It's not as if she didn't want Kira to hear, it was more a matter of her honoring the intimacy of the two of us moving and breathing together. While we took our three steps sideways, the utterly wrong thought that came to me was that *this* was what we were doing instead of inviting Kira to watch us have sex. I stifled my impulse to say aloud, *I much prefer this to that.*

"Gertrude. Isabelle. Tasha. Annie." Maura tapped the glass of each picture with the nail of her forefinger. "My cousins." Those names, too, she meant for Kira to hear. And she must have intended the photos and our dance as a way to give Kira some background for what we were about to demonstrate for her when we escorted her into the study with us. A necessary preparation.

"Now a loop and twirl," Maura murmured. "Slowly, please."

Oh, I knew that move so well I felt a little burst of vanity in performing for Kira.

We ended up exactly where we were supposed to, standing up straight and side by side, each with an arm around the other's waist. Maura trusted me to take the next set of moves from memory—forward two steps and two to the right. Then we were facing the old man who gave Maura her first lesson in death administration.

"Grandpa Durham," she announced as if our audience were an entire room full of people rather than a single small young woman with her eyes alert as a wild animal's.

Kira stood up from the table. Slowly and deliberately she stepped toward us. When she was near enough to us for us to feel her breathing, she turned and took her place in front of and slightly to the side of Maura. Stair-stepped like children of a family—me, Maura, then Kira—the three of us stood before the belligerent-faced old man.

Kira's voice was very soft. "A small question," she said. Maura and I stayed quiet.

"Did you kill my old boss?" She kept her voice so low it was as if she thought we were sleeping and she didn't want to wake us up. "Did you kill my Uncle Jimmy?"

She had her back turned to us, and we could barely hear her. She probably hadn't wanted to ask us those questions, and Maura and I were certainly smart enough to know she didn't want to hear our answers. We stayed quiet.

In a moment, Kira stepped away and turned to face us. "It's okay," she said with a little smile. "You don't have to tell me."

END GAME

Maura's sense of purpose had been restored by our alliance with Kira, and I believed that once we sat down at her desk she would naturally assume her role as the one of us who forked the lightning. Until that moment, though, I thought it was appropriate for me to be the one who led the way to the door and opened it.

Maura entered first, signaling Kira to follow her. I brought in a chair from the kitchen table and placed it between the two chairs at the desk. Maura pushed it back a little, so that she and I wouldn't be quite so separated by Kira's presence. I appreciated that because I hadn't figured out how we should arrange ourselves in the room. When I closed the door, I noticed Kira looking at me quizzically.

"I'm not sure why we do," I told her, "but we always close the door."

Maura was studying the notes she had taken with the information from Kira, and her fingers were already speeding along. "I'll get them both identified and located," she told Kira. "That'll take a few minutes, but then we can do one and then the other pretty quickly."

Kira watched Maura's fingers, of course, but I quickly noticed that she gave most of her attention to the monitor in front of us. The screens on the monitor changed so quickly that I had long ago given up trying to understand them and instead allowed myself to become entranced by the quick agility of those fingers. Now I wondered if Kira was sophisticated enough to follow the steps of Maura's process. I remembered that when I first entered this room with Maura, she had made an effort to explain to me what she was doing, but she wasn't doing that with Kira. In my case, she'd known that I was such a technological dunce I could grasp only a non-technical description of what she did. She even mentioned the deployment of a drone so tiny it couldn't be detected by any device that had yet been invented. It made me anxious even to imagine such a deadly little thing. With Kira, however, it was not out of the question that she could be learning a great deal of the technology just from keeping her eyes on the screens as they flashed before our eyes. In any case, such thinking seemed to me a violation of my agreement with Maura to pretend-trust Kira even if actual trust wasn't possible.

The three of us descended into such quietness that we might have been attending a percussion concert with Maura Nelson performing the First Unaccompanied Suite for Mac Pro 12 Keyboard. When it seemed to be going on far too long, I reminded myself that she was preparing for two transitions. Also, the quiet and the rapid bursts of clicking of the keyboard were soothing enough. I could probably have waited like that until daylight.

Finally, Maura heaved a tremendous sigh and leaned back in her chair. "God, I thought I would never get that right!" she said, looking first at me then at Kira. She closed her eyes a moment, then sat forward and slid the mouse to a point that was exactly between the two of us and directly in front of Kira, who was sitting back far enough that she wouldn't be able to reach it unless she moved her chair forward or stood up and bent forward between Maura and me.

Maura leaned back in her chair again, clasped her hands behind her head and turned her eyes up to the ceiling as if she was about to speak to God. "They're all set to go," she said.

⌘

I wasn't going to be the one who reached for that mouse first, and I was pretty sure it wasn't going to be Maura. My guess was that she wanted to give Kira the opportunity to volunteer—and she thought it was fine that Kira was somewhat baffled in that moment. All the better to see what the girl revealed or didn't reveal in this crucial situation.

Kira seemed to have stopped breathing, and her face had gone so pale she looked like she had been embalmed. It must have been close to 3 in the morning. I knew that Maura was exhausted from the concentration it had taken to prepare the way for Yury and Pyotr, and I was so far past my bedtime that I worried I might fall asleep in my chair. But I was so determined to see how the situation played out that I was aware of my heartbeat.

What do you want me to do?

Kira's words floated so softly into the silence around us that they seemed more a mental transmission than spoken language.

"Single click. That will be Pyotr. Then wait while I change the setting to Yury, which will take only a moment. I'll tell you when to click for him." Maura's voice was notably calm.

Kira stood and leaned forward. She clicked once. Then Maura sat up straight and keyed in the information for Yury. Kira hardly paused before she clicked the mouse a second time. When she sat back down, I noticed that her face was suffused with color. For a moment the three of us sat without moving.

"Dead?" whispered Kira.

"Dead," Maura said. "Both of them."

⌘

Maura and I moved like zombies into the living room with Kira following along behind. She appeared to be caught up in her thoughts. Maura went with Kira into the little apartment. From our bedroom I heard the murmur of their talking, Kira's voice notably animated. I was almost asleep when Maura slipped into bed with me. "Long day tomorrow," she whispered. "She wants to do all the ones she told us about this evening." She snuggled in close with me. "I'm not sure how she's taking this, Jack—she seems fine, but I think maybe it's hard on her, too. She probably doesn't realize that yet."

"Hard to know what she's feeling," I said. "But my sense was that she felt pretty good after she'd clicked that mouse on old Pyotr and Yury." I whispered, too, though I doubted Kira could hear us even if our voices had been raised.

"Maybe," Maura said. I was almost asleep when I

thought I heard her whisper, "But I think some of them are her own family."

I was awake first and full of energy. I wanted to make the morning an occasion. I had done this a few times when my kids were little and Vicki and I still thought we could aspire to a more or less normal American life. I might as well have gone ahead and said, "happy," because those were the days when Annette Funicello and Frankie Avalon and Elvis were making beach movies. Our family breakfasts were sufficiently chaotic to add plenty of comedy to the morning even if full-fledged happiness never quite made it to the table. At any rate, I went out early to buy eggs and sausage and bacon and English muffins, and I had the table set and everything ready when Kira peeked in from her apartment door. When I asked her to go wake up Maura, the girl smiled at me like a sleepy kid.

Of course Maura gave me quite the skeptical look when she first stepped out of our bedroom. "I couldn't imagine why I might be smelling bacon when I woke up," she said. "I was sure I was dreaming." When she saw the feast I had prepared, the look on her face wasn't easy to translate. "I swear, Jack, I never could have predicted you would do anything like this." There was no irony in her voice. The moment might even have qualified as a tender one.

So we ate heartily, Maura and I making small talk with Kira about her job in the kitchen at the museum and where she found places to sleep. Kira wasn't especially forthcoming, but our questions made her smile wryly at us. "You're very interested in this, aren't you?" she said. "Aren't Americans sort of…?" She waggled her hand to suggest, I suppose, that we were comfortable with the many homeless people we had on the streets of all our towns and cities.

"I guess we are," I said.

"I wish we weren't," Maura said.

Kira shrugged, as if it made little difference to her what we thought about our homeless population.

When we had eaten all we wanted, we didn't linger at the table. The three of us stood up and pitched in on the clean-up. I wondered if maybe some kind of American farm-life ethos had sifted down into our apartment and filtered into our brains. But as the kitchen became cleaner and tidier, we had less and less to say. Maura and I found ourselves leaning back against the counter, watching Kira while she sat at the table looking around the apartment but not meeting our eyes.

Then she looked directly first at Maura then at me. She smiled and tilted her head toward the study door. "In there?" she asked. "Yes?" she asked.

When Maura and I nodded, she stood up.

We followed her in.

⌘

In the room we took on the daunting task of identifying and precisely locating men in small cities of Russia, Hungary, Bulgaria, Croatia, Serbia, and Romania. As we worked we sat side by side, pressed right up against the desk, and occasionally touching each other's elbows or hands. I read Maura's notes aloud, then worked with

Maura to find the approximate location of each individual. All three of us had to puzzle out the alternative spellings of a name. So it took us two and a half hours to locate and identify Yefim Levkov. But then finally the moment arrived when Maura relinquished the mouse and leaned back in her chair.

With no hesitation whatsoever, Kira reached forward, placed her hand on the device, muttered something in Russian, and clicked it.

"What did you say?" I asked.

Kira turned to me with her face red and her eyes wide open. Then, shockingly, she put her hand over her mouth and giggled. "I said, 'Go burn your dick off in hell, Yefim Yurivich.'" She looked from me to Maura then back to me. "Is that all right?" she asked.

Maura and I caught each other's eyes before we, too, laughed. It felt both wrong and right. "I think that's a splendid way to say goodbye to Yefim," Maura said.

The concentration and effort Yefim Yurivich Levkov had required of us seemed so enormous that it made all the kills Maura and I had carried out seem easy as a children's computer game. Even so, I could tell that Maura was entirely ready to move on to the next man on Kira's list. Kira appeared to be trying to contain her eagerness to keep going. The fact that this was Kira's list and not ours seemed to liberate and revitalize Maura and me. We had days of work ahead of us, but if Kira was going to bid farewell to each of them by saying, "Go burn your dick off in hell," I knew I would carry on cheerfully. The kid had brought a new spirit into the room.

⌘

Arseny Chepelski, Vyacheslav Dvorkin, Gleb Gusarov, Dmitry Iskander, Yefim Khavin, Mikhail Shtadler, Evegeny Nisselovich, Immanuil Pletner, Kirill Rosenthal, Lev Petrowa, Makar Bobrov, Nestor Semenov, Oleg Oborski, Mikhail Buryskin, and Roman Gepfner: At first Maura and I were grateful that we knew nothing about those people and that we only had to think of them as men whom Kira knew to be sex traffickers. It helped that their names—though completely familiar to Kira—were foreign to Maura and me. We didn't know if they had wives or children or if they possessed any redeeming qualities. We assumed they were rich from their business of buying and selling young girls and boys from extremely poor families. It also helped us to remember Uncle Jimmy when we thought of those men.

"We have four more to go," Maura told me one evening in the second week as we were undressing for bed. When she slipped her nightgown down over her head, she laughed a little bitterly and grimaced. "It's like our job, isn't it? All day we work on killing bad guys. Then we eat and go to bed."

She stood still and stared at me, though I couldn't read her face very well.

"Sometimes we have sex," I said. I didn't say that to be funny, but I suppose it was. I wasn't ready to tell Maura that the whole situation felt different to me now that Kira had joined us in the transition room.

Maura's smile was small and a little pinched. "That helps some," she said.

⌘

It had taken us nearly a month to move through Kira's list. We had had to cross off two men we simply couldn't locate—Oleg Oborski and Dmitri Iskander. Eventually Nestor Semenov was our last remaining candidate, and we'd worked through the morning and beyond lunchtime trying to determine that this man was not anywhere in Russia or Europe but had been working out of Bangkok for the past six months. Once we knew where he was, generally, it took Maura only another half hour to determine his precise location. Around 3:45 of that Friday afternoon Maura nodded to signal to us that Nestor was very nearly all set to begin his ultimate journey.

When Maura slid the mouse over to its usual place, Kira immediately clicked Nestor Semenov into oblivion. But for the first time she had nothing to say. She sat without moving, as if she had clicked herself into catatonia. She stared at her hand still holding the mouse.

Maura and I knew something was troubling her. The room stayed quiet. We waited. We were very tired from the effort we had invested in Nestor, but from the look on Maura's face I knew that she didn't want us to stand up and leave Kira sitting here. If she would have just taken her hand away from the mouse, that would probably have released us.

I noticed that Kira's mouth was set tight and her jaw was twitching. Only slightly but enough to notice if you were studying her. Maura's hand moved to the girl's shoulder.

"What?" Maura asked softly. "What's wrong, Kira?"

Kira suddenly pushed the mouse away and sat up straight as if she meant for Maura to stop touching her.

Maura took her hand away but continued to look at the girl with concern.

"Two more names," Kira said in a harsh voice that was far too loud for that small room with its door closed. She sat still with her eyes slitted.

"All right," I said, taking my cue from Maura to speak softly. I picked up a pen and moved the list in front me so as to be able to add the two new names.

"Timur Komarovski," Kira said, her voice raspy and again too loud. She was blinking and her face was red. Then, as if she were about to vomit, she blurted, "Galenka Komarovski!"

Maura moved her chair as close as she could to Kira and carefully put her arms around the girl. The girl allowed it. Maura gave me a nod to suggest that I should leave the room.

I closed the door behind me. And waited in the living room. I could hear Kira's voice rising and falling, though I couldn't make out what she was saying. And I heard the murmur of Maura's speaking to her softly. After a few minutes I picked up the new issue of *The New York Review of Books*, but of course I couldn't really concentrate. In a few more minutes Kira stopped speaking, and then I heard Maura's fingers on the keyboard.

I couldn't help thinking about the new names Kira had given us. Galenka Komarovski was the first woman she had ever named to her list, and since she shared a last name with the other person, it was likely they were brother and sister or husband and wife. And Kira wouldn't have been so wrought up about adding them to her list if there weren't.... If they weren't....

Maura stepped out of her office and closed the door behind her—leaving Kira in there. She walked to the sofa and sat beside me, very close. "They're her parents," she told me in her quietest voice. "She wants to do them now."

She registered my question without my having to ask it.

"She's afraid she might change her mind if we don't act now," she told me.

"Okay," I said.

"She says they sold her. She says she overheard them haggling over the selling price. The buyers wanted to pay less for Kira because she was only nine years old." Maura examined my face, and I imagined what it revealed to her—a nauseated horror over parents who would sell a daughter. "She says that her parents knew they were entitled to more money. Nine-year-olds were more valuable than the older ones."

In a moment Maura said, "I have them ready to go."

"She wants me in there when she does it?" I asked.

"Yes and no," Maura said. She offered a grim little smile.

I waited.

"Yes, she wants you in there."

"And the no?"

"She doesn't want to do the clicks. She wants you to do them."

This news made me wince—and I knew Maura had known how I would respond. She gave me a little shrug.

"I told her I'd ask you," she said.

I was so stunned I couldn't think clearly. After a moment I asked, "What if I say no?"

Maura shrugged and looked away from me. "I guess Timur and Galenka will remain among the living," she said.

I waited for more.

"You can understand why Kira wouldn't want to do it?"

"Well, not really," I said. "But on the other hand, my parents never tried to sell me. So far as I know."

"It's me you're wondering about, isn't it? Why can't I do it? That's what you want to know?"

"I guess so. I mean yes, that's what I want to know."

"I'm not sure. All I know is that when Kira said she couldn't do it herself, I was completely certain I couldn't do it. Kill her parents. I'm sorry. It's just not in me to do it."

"I understand," I said. My brain felt broken. I had very little appetite for killing Kira's parents. But evidently I had less ambivalence than Kira did. And if they did what she said they did, sold her into... sold her into slavery. That's what it was, and in this regard, there was no difference between Timur and Galenka and those men we'd been executing during these past weeks. On the sofa arm beside me was the piece of paper on which I had added the new names a few moments ago. Kira's list. The girl gave us these names of people she knew to be deeply evil, and Maura and I set forth on a murdering spree. All over the planet men literally dropped in their tracks, because in the wildly random distribution of contemporary technological power, Maura and I had come to possess the capacity to do this. A piece of paper with forty-six names.

A year ago I wouldn't have thought myself capable of such thinking. I was stricken with an extreme regard for Kira. And not because she was a good person. Only in this one particular way—she had it in her to strike back at people who had done harm to her—could she possibly be considered good. The girl had sufficient fire in her to kill her parents. Only in the Old Testament could this be considered admirable. And if I understood my feelings at that moment, I had suddenly lurched over into desire. I had known for a long time that I was drawn to competent women, women who could take action. If I made a list of the women who had affected me this way, Maura would of course be at the top, but right now Kira would have been there beside her.

In college I used to get crushes on some of the waitresses in the places where I ate. When I figured out it was because they were good at what they did, that insight did not prevent me from getting stupid crushes. It just made me expand my range. I found myself attracted to bank tellers, store clerks, my Con Law teacher Professor Dineger, and God help me, women musicians. I mean real musicians, not just rockers and screamers with great voices, but those with training and taste. Like Julie London, who was probably old enough to be my great grandmother. Swear to God I could probably still get an erection if I heard that woman singing "Cry Me a River."

There never was a good excuse for my seguing from admiration into what Mr. Springsteen called "a bad desire," but this with Kira was taking it too far. At least now I was old enough to see what was going on in my beasty interior life. Being desired by me was absolutely the last thing Kira needed in her life.

"All right, Maura," I told her. "I'll do it," I said, "even though all three of us may regret this. I have it in me," I said.

Surely she could hear what I was really saying—*I'm strong enough to do what you can't.* But I certainly hoped she couldn't hear any signal that I was willing to click that mouse twice just so Kira would see me in a more favorable light.

I stood up. So did Maura. But I was the one who led the way back into the study.

⌘

Maura was making sandwiches for dinner. Kira and I sat opposite each other in the living room. All three of us were keeping our thoughts to ourselves. I had my eyes directed toward the *New York Review of Books* on my lap, but my brain had stalled out. So far as I could tell, Kira's eyes were directed toward Maura in the kitchen. Our excuse for not talking was that Maura had turned on the radio to hear the news on NPR. The news was all about the bombs that had killed and maimed people at the Boston Marathon. Last night they had captured the youngest of the two bombers, the nineteen-year-old boy who came to America when he was eight years old.

Maura stepped into the living room to signal that our food was ready.

Before I sat down I thought to ask, "Wine?"

Maura and Kira had taken their places at the table. They shook their heads.

So then I sat down with them, but immediately another thought came to me. "Whiskey?" I asked. I meant the offer mostly as a joke.

Maura looked shocked and bemused.

Kira slowly turned her head toward me. Then she nodded. "Yes, please," she said. Her face might have been trying to tell me something.

When I had first moved in with Maura, I brought with me a bottle of eighteen-year-old Jefferson's Presidential Select Bourbon, a gift from Bobby Jenkins, my broker, the previous year for Christmas. Now I stood up again, found the whiskey, and brought it to the table. From the cabinet over the sink, I selected three juice glasses and set them on the table beside the bottle.

"Ice?" I asked.

Both ladies shook their heads. So I sat down, twisted the top off the bottle, and poured two fingers worth into each glass. It occurred to me that this whiskey might be older than Kira. And that I was probably breaking the law by providing alcohol to a minor.

Maura looked at each of us, then lifted her glass. I lifted mine, too, and when Kira lifted hers I suddenly understood what her face was telling me. *See what I can do? My blood is even colder than yours.*

I was staggered by that message, and I thought my face probably showed it. Even so, I kept my glass raised politely. Since Maura had started this, I expected her to speak, but she shook her head at me. I started to shake my own head, then I decided that when an hour earlier I had clicked the mouse twice and stopped the hearts of Kira's parents, I had forfeited my right to say no to anything these women wanted of me.

I had in mind to say *Cheers*, but what came out of my mouth was, "To a world where we can be our true selves."

We clinked. Then we drank. Kira and I tossed ours

down. Maura made a face with her first sip, but then she, too, turned up her glass and finished it. Made another face.

All three of us set our glasses together in the center of the table. I poured two more fingers for each of us.

HELL PAYS A VISIT

Our bedroom door opened not quite silently, sending a quick slice of light over Maura asleep beside me. I could have been dreaming. A shadow entered, then the door closed and the room went dark again. The clock on my bedside table said 1:30. When the shadow slid under the covers beside Maura I decided it was either dream-Kira or real-Kira, and whichever it was I was fine with her being in there. If it was real-Kira, then I had to admire her nerve, but I was also aware of Mr. Jefferson's whiskey in my system, having its way with my thoughts. When Maura stirred, I turned on my side facing away from her. I wanted to burrow deeper into my sleep, but I was too stirred up to manage it right away.

I did, however, drift off into a kind of half sleep, during which I became aware of some quiet rustling and body movement on Maura's side of the bed. I decided Kira's entering our room was what a little kid will do when she's had a nightmare and runs to her parents' room to crawl in with them and be reassured by their bodies. This was all right, I thought—I'd killed the most important people in Kira's life, and so of course she needed to know that Maura and I were here for her. In my half sleep I realized that she was now lying between Maura and me, and I reached over to comfort her.

When my hand transmitted to me that the place it had landed was Kira's small, bare breast, my mind started rising toward waking. But it did not instruct the hand to move away or even to find another place to land. If anything, my coming into consciousness complicated the matter. My hand was happy where it was and my palm was all a-twitter because it thought Kira's nipple might be colluding. Furthermore, I couldn't help remembering Kira's turning her face to me during our toast. This was indeed a woman who in these past weeks had shown a zest for killing that exceeded my own. And who this very day had sentenced her parents to the death penalty, courtesy of my willingness to click the mouse on them. Had we not already been conniving? Perhaps Mr. Jefferson's whiskey informed my reasoning, but I couldn't help posing the question—in the face of that level of wrongful behavior, what was a hand on a breast?

My brain had also taken up the question of whether Maura could be asleep or unconscious with Kira and me about to do some heavy petting only inches away from her. Would Maura pretend to be asleep? Would she consider this to be a variation of pretend-trust? My brain debated the issues. Meanwhile my body carried out its agenda.

I snuggled closer to Kira and gave the breast-touching hand permission to move downward over her skin. If she had worn any clothing when she entered this room, she must have taken it off. And at the same time my hand slid over her pubic bone, I felt her hand searching my pajama bottoms for an opening.

That she wanted me, too, exhilarated me, so to clear the way for Kira's hand I lurched my hips around clumsily, thereby shaking the bed in a very obvious and stupid way.

Maura lifted herself up, switched on her bedside light, turned her head and helped herself to the vision of Kira and me with our hands on each other.

Kira's eyes opened wide, she blinked in the sudden light, and she appeared to be jolted awake. This would forever be a question I would ask myself. Was she really asleep and dreaming about some fantasy lover, or was she truly getting sexual with me? Maybe my thinking that the latter was an actual possibility meant that I was desperate to hold onto my self-esteem. It didn't matter. Only a few seconds passed before her face twisted itself into maybe the angriest expression I'd ever seen on a human face, and she backhanded me hard across the mouth.

I half stumbled and half fell out of the bed with my lower lip spouting blood. Kira was naked and spitting curses. Maura's pajama top was half unbuttoned, and the two of them were trying to untangle themselves from the bedcovers. The room was a nightmare.

Then Kira sprang out of my side of the bed, bent over where I lay on the floor, shouted at me in Russian, spat in my face, and swung a fist at me that barely missed. She seemed to fly out through the bedroom door, slamming it so hard that it felt like an explosion. In my future obsessive re-runs of this scene, she deliberately missed me with that swing of her fist. I hoped she'd meant that one as a show for Maura's benefit.

I used the side of the bed to pull myself up, and Maura and I faced each other and blinked in the light. We could have been strangers who'd been flung into that room from outer space.

⌘

My brain processed dozens of possible sentences. What came out of my bloody mouth in that moment was, "*Go burn your dick off in hell.* I could be wrong, but I think that's what she said."

Maura waited a moment, evidently considering what I'd told her. Then she nodded. "Yes, that's probably right." Her voice sounded sleep-muffled, mutated—the words of someone who had just survived a car wreck.

I pulled off a pillow case and pressed it to my lip.

⌘

We heard Kira's stomping around the apartment. She had on boots or heavy shoes that made her footsteps sound like those of a giant. We heard thumps and crashes. Things breaking. Dishes, lamps, a chair kicked across the room.

"Should I go out there?" I asked.

Maura was lying on the bed, under the covers with the back of her hand shading her eyes. We heard more harsh footsteps and a heavy clattering that must have been the appliances from the kitchen counter being swept off onto the floor.

I had my hand on the door, ready to go out there and try to persuade Kira to calm down.

"No, don't," Maura finally said very faintly. "Better that she do her damage to us now rather than later."

I was very relieved that I didn't have to go out there and deal with Kira's rage. With the pillow case pressed to my mouth I turned off the bedside light, lay down and pulled the covers up over my shoulders.

We heard Kira bang the door of Maura's study against the wall right next to our bedroom. It was loud as a gunshot. Then that room went quiet. And stayed quiet.

It was silent a long time. Maura's breathing suggested she had fallen asleep. I meant to stay awake, but I didn't manage it.

The huge slamming of the door to Maura's apartment startled both of us awake. I sat up in bed to wait for what came next, but it was only Kira's heavy footsteps going down the staircase. Then the slamming of the door downstairs.

The bedside clock informed me that it was ten minutes till six. I remembered that this was a Saturday morning.

⌘

Eventually I forced myself up out of bed. It took a while for me to will myself from sitting on the side of the bed up to a standing position. I knew Maura wasn't really asleep, but the very fact of her stillness told me she didn't want conversation. I picked up yesterday's pants and shirt from the floor and put them on. I slipped my feet into my bedroom slippers.

Even though I had heard the noises Kira made, when I opened the bedroom door I was astonished at the wreckage she was able to inflict. Lamps, vases, picture frames—anything that was breakable had been broken. Whatever was throwable she had flung it. If she'd had an axe she'd have chopped up the chairs, the tables, and the sofa. Something had been tossed out through the window glass through which we had observed so many birds in the limbs of the tree outside. I chose not to look out there to see what Kira used to break the glass.

The kitchen table lay on its side. Dishes, glasses, pots,

skillets, cups, flatware, appliances—it had all been thrown to the floor. Broken pieces of everything were all mixed together. Beside the sink, in a cleared space, were the ripped-up pieces of something I had to study a few moments before I could identify what they might have been. Then it came to me: they were the two photographs of Maura and me that we had placed side by side a month ago. And beside them, like an offering of some kind, was a matchbook with one unstruck match torn loose and lying beside it. I studied that, too, because it clearly seemed a message, but not one that I understood.

It was that little arrangement that I showed to Maura when she did finally emerge from the bedroom. Part of why I did so was to distract her from the overall catastrophe that was her apartment. She stared at the torn-up photos and the matches for some time before she shook her head and said, "She's telling us she could have set the place on fire but didn't."

"Burned us alive," I murmured.

Maura nodded and studied Kira's message a while longer. Then she bowed her head and slowly walked back to the bedroom. She didn't close the door, but she did lie down under the bedcovers. She picked up a book from the stack on her bedside table; she arranged her pillows so that she could prop the book up to read it.

All that day we behaved like survivors. Maura evidently intended to spend the day in the bedroom, which was fine with me. She didn't mind if I occasionally went in to tell her or ask her something. I was sure she wasn't reading, but I understood the need to hold one's self in a trance in order to get through a time of extreme difficulty.

We didn't even discuss the idea of leaving the apartment. Painful as it was to view the enormous wreckage Kira had left us, it was equally disturbing to consider how we would manage the clean-up. When I had gotten my lip to stop bleeding, I puttered a little, mostly moving things aside to make a path. I stood or paced or went in and sat on my side of the bed, then paced some more. Maura and I could hardly bring ourselves to speak, though when we did, we chose our words carefully and with maximum consideration for the other person. I told her that Kira didn't think to throw the food out of the refrigerator; when I asked her if she'd like me to bring her some juice she said yes, she would like that.

It was while I was in the kitchen trying to find an unbroken glass that I heard Maura's soft "Oh" from the bedroom. I turned to see her leaving the bedroom and moving in the direction of her study. I, too, had forgotten it. The door was pulled to, but it wasn't latched. When Maura pushed it open, I followed her in.

At first the room looked to be just as we left it yesterday—yesterday!—evening. Then I heard Maura's sharp inhaling gasp. When I turned I saw she had her hand to her mouth and she was gazing at the backsides of her two main computers turned to face us on the desk with their innards exposed. The two rear panels lay beside the machines with their screws scattered beside them. Right beside the panels was Maura's small flashlight on the desk, placed as if Kira wanted Maura to find it there.

Maura carefully sat down, picked up the flashlight, and inspected the opened-up cases of her computers. Almost immediately she leaned back in her chair. I expected her to look at me, but she didn't. She blinked straight ahead at the machines. "She took the hard drives," she murmured.

CODA

When I think of it now, our leave-taking seems to have happened in an hour or two. But of course it actually took a couple of weeks. I helped Maura deal with the wreckage and move the apartment back toward a state where she might live in it until she could find another place. But that first night after Kira's departure we discovered we could hardly bear to be in the same bed with each other. Instead of moving toward the middle after we were both under the covers, we each migrated to opposite sides—and then tossed and turned when we'd switched out the lights. After an hour or so Maura apologized and took her pillows and a blanket out to the sofa. And the next night I took my turn sleeping in the wrecked living room. We took care not to touch each other even though we were very polite in what we had to say.

We didn't discuss that change in our feelings for each other, because it was just so clear and final: As far as we were concerned we'd transitioned desire out of our lives. I couldn't bring myself to ask Maura if she'd lain there watching me reaching over and fondling the girl's breast. Or to ask her if there'd been any sex between the two of them before Kira moved over between us. I know this was cowardly of me, but the truth is I knew I'd rather live without either of those questions being answered. I would argue that it takes a peculiar form of strength to carry on one's life by way of deliberate ignorance.

I offered to pay for professional cleaners to come in to deal with the damage, but Maura said she'd rather I just help her carry the broken and ruined things out to the dumpster of her apartment complex and give her a hand with tidying the place up. She said she'd tell me what she wanted, and I was happy enough to oblige her. Even then, though we hadn't yet said it aloud, we knew we were finished. Or we knew that Maura was moving somewhere else and that I was not going with her.

What was especially peculiar about the situation was that the desire to separate was both equal and cordial. I attribute this easiness to the explosion Kira set off in our bedroom, a violence that now seems to me oddly commensurate with the murderous path Maura and I had followed together all those months. It was as if she and I had been friendly acquaintances who'd been thrown together by chance, and now we were free to go our own ways. To be frank, our splitting up was the easiest part of our whole time together. For me the move was weirdly trouble-free because all I had to do was pack a couple of suitcases and drive back to my place. Which had been waiting for me all the while. It felt like a college hook-up that hadn't worked out.

I sometimes ask myself if I'm lonely, and my answer is usually, "A little." But even then I wonder if what I'm really lonely for is the killing we did. In those days when we walked into Maura's study to carry out a transition, I felt so alive I was almost giddy. In my sleepy life nowadays I have trouble believing I was ever that person. A man who could kill another man and feel fine about it. Feel like I'd accomplished something worthwhile.

What I've decided to think about my year and two months with Maura is that she and I fell into our death-delivering ways by accident. And I believe that it was also a random happening that Kira came to us and stayed long enough to enable us to kill more than a dozen strangers scattered around the world. And finally, of course, she delivered us back to our proper selves. Thanks to Kira, Maura and I were born again. In our final days together we were not the man and woman who had bonded powerfully and destructively in that apartment. When Kira ripped up those photographs of us in our youth, she must have enacted some kind of spell that threw us back to the lives we should have had all along.

Of course I think about Maura every day, and in an abstract way I miss her. We both agreed that I didn't need her "contact information," as it is called these days. She said that even though she wasn't leaving DC or her job, she was going to try to keep such a low profile she'd be very nearly invisible. "I think you should do the same, Jack," she told me. "Live small," she said. I told her that I thought this would probably happen without my trying.

So in the last hours I spent in Maura's apartment we agreed that we owed each other nothing. I don't think it hurt the feelings of either of us that what we wanted was not to see the other one ever again. That afternoon we were quietly drinking tea when the idea came to me to lift my cup to Maura without having thought about what I might say. I meant the gesture to be one of profound appreciation of her—of my gratitude, as it were. But since I said nothing, I know she didn't take the gesture that way.

She lifted her cup, too. "To the end," she said and smiled. It was a somewhat rueful smile, but she seemed to have recovered her old strength. I touched my cup to hers and fully intended to repeat her toast aloud. Remembering it now, I'm sure that I mouthed the words, *To the end*, but I'm not certain I actually said them aloud.

When I finished my tea and stood up to walk to the door, I saw her start to stand up, too. I suddenly imagined us stepping toward her door in that eerie unison that we'd discovered in our first weeks together. God help me, I even envisioned Maura and me making a detour back to her study and the two of us locating and identifying Ned Ruse and Nelson Graham and Henry Gohmert and... By Jesus I wanted just one more click to send that preposterous lying twit Marcelle Halbgehirn to the heaven she was sure was waiting for her.

Another train of thinking came to me in that moment, and it wasn't nearly so welcome as the fantasy of Maura and me picking up where we'd left off. This vision was of Maura rebuilding her computer system, reprogramming her machines to recover her lost power. I saw her entering her study one morning in the future, allowing her fingers their ritual dance over the keyboard as they tracked down and identified me. I saw her sensible face. I saw her moving the mouse to its place directly in front of her and taking a deep breath before she single-clicked it.

But then I saw Maura's body relax back into her chair and her face signal that she'd changed her mind about walking me to the door.

"Take care," she said with a friendly goodbye lift of her hand.

"You, too," I said.

ACKNOWLEDGMENTS

The first chapter of this novel ("The Future") appeared in *Agni 76*.